D1180589

FIVE ON A SECRET TRAIL

Enid Blyton's

FIVE ON A
SECRET TRAIL

ILLUSTRATED BY JOLYNE KNOX

AWARD PUBLICATIONS

ISBN 0-86163-600-7

First published 1956 by Hodder and Stoughton Ltd
This edition 1985

This edition first published 1992 by Award Publications
Limited, 1st Floor, Goodyear House, 52–56 Osnaburgh Street,
London NW1 3NS

Printed in Finland

CONTENTS

1 George is rather difficult   7
2 Anne joins the little camp   14
3 The old cottage – and a surprise   21
4 That night   28
5 That boy again!   35
6 Storm in the night   43
7 Queer happenings   51
8 All together again!   59
9 A little exploration   67
10 What can be happening?   74
11 Interesting discoveries – and a plan   82
12 A good hiding-place   89
13 On watch in the cottage   96
14 An exciting night – and a surprising morning   103
15 Well done, George!   111
16 The secret way   118
17 Full of surprises   125
18 The way out   133
19 Back to Kirrin Cottage   141
20 The adventure ends – as it began!   148

1

George is Rather Difficult

'Mother! Mother, where are you?' shouted George, rushing into the house. 'Mother, quick!'

There was no answer. George's mother was out in the garden at the back of Kirrin Cottage, picking flowers. George yelled again, this time at the top of her very strong voice.

'MOTHER! MOTHER! Where are you? IT's URGENT.'

A door was flung open nearby and George's father stood there, glaring at her.

'George! What's this row about? Here am I in the middle of some very difficult . . .'

'Oh Father! Timmy's hurt!' said George. 'He went . . .'

Her father looked down at Timmy, standing meekly behind George. He gave a little snort.

'Hurt! He seems all right to me. I suppose he's got a thorn in his paw again – and you think it's the end of the world or something, and come yelling in here and . . .'

'Timmy *is* hurt!' said George, with tears in her voice. 'Look!'

But her father had gone back into his study again, and the door slammed. George glared at it, looking exactly like her hot-tempered father.

'You're unkind!' she shouted, 'and . . . oh there's MOTHER. MOTHER!'

'Dear me, George, whatever *is* the matter?' said her mother, putting down the flowers. 'I heard your father shouting, and then you.'

'Mother – Timmy's hurt!' said George. 'Look!'

She knelt down by the dog, and gently pulled forward one ear. Behind it was a big cut. Timmy whined. Tears came into George's eyes, and she looked up at her mother.

'Now don't be silly, George,' said Mrs Kirrin. 'It's only a cut. How did he do it?'

'He tried to jump over a ditch, and he didn't see some old barbed wire there,' said George. 'And a rusty piece caught his ear, and ripped that awful cut. I can't stop it bleeding.'

Her mother looked at it. It certainly was quite deep. 'Take him to the vet, George,' she said. 'Perhaps it ought to be stitched. It does look rather deep. Poor old Timmy-boy – well, it's a good thing it wasn't his eye, George.'

'I'll take him to the vet at once,' said George, getting up. 'Will he be in, Mother?'

'Oh yes – it's his surgery hour,' said her mother. 'Take him along now.'

So Timmy was hurried along the country lanes to the pretty little house where the vet lived. George, very anxious indeed, was most relieved to see that the vet seemed quite unconcerned.

'A couple of stitches and that cut will heal well,' he said. 'Hold him, will you, while I do the job? He'll hardly feel it. There, old boy – stand still – that's right.'

In five minutes' time George was thanking the vet

wholeheartedly. 'Thank you! I *was* worried! Will he be all right now?'

'Good gracious, yes – but you mustn't let him scratch that wound,' said the vet, washing his hands. 'If he does, it may go wrong.'

'Oh. But how can I stop him?' asked George anxiously. 'Look – he's trying to scratch it now.'

'Well, you must make him a big cardboard collar,' said the vet. 'One that sticks out right round his neck, so that his paw can't get near that cut, however much he tries to reach it.'

'But – but Timmy won't like that a bit,' said George. 'Dogs look silly wearing cardboard collars like great ruffs round their neck. I've seen them. He'll hate one.'

'Well, it's the only way of stopping him from scratching that wound,' said the vet. 'Get along now, George – I've more patients waiting.'

George went home with Timmy. He padded along quietly, pleased at the fuss that George was making of him. When he was nearly home, he suddenly sat down and put up his hind leg to scratch his bad ear.

'No, Timmy! NO!' cried George, in alarm. 'You must NOT scratch. You'll get the plaster off in no time, and break the stitches. NO, Timmy!'

Timmy looked up in surprise. Very well. If scratching was suddenly upsetting George, he would wait till he was alone.

But George could read Timmy's thoughts as easily as he could read hers! She frowned.

'Blow! I'll *have* to make him that cardboard collar. Perhaps Mother will help me.'

Her mother was quite willing to help. George was not good at things of that sort, and she watched her mother cutting out a big cardboard collar, fitting it round the surprised Timmy's head, and then lacing the edges together with thread so that he could not get it off. Timmy was most surprised, but he stood very patiently.

As soon as the collar was finished, and safely round his neck, he walked away. Then he raised his hind leg to scratch at his smarting ear – but, of course, he couldn't get it over the collar, and merely scratched the cardboard.

'Never mind, Timmy,' said George. 'It will only be for a few days.'

The study door nearby opened and her father came out. He saw Timmy in his collar and stopped in surprise. Then he roared with laughter.

'Hey, Timmy – you look like Queen Elizabeth the First in a fine big ruff!' he said.

'Don't laugh at him, Father,' said George. 'You know that dogs can't bear being laughed at.'

Timmy certainly looked offended. He turned his back on George's father and stalked off to the kitchen. A little squeal of laughter came from there and then a loud guffaw from someone at the kitchen door – the milkman.

'Oh Timmy – whatever have you got that collar on for?' said the cook's voice. 'You do look peculiar!'

George was angry. She remained angry all that day and made everyone most uncomfortable. How *mean* of people to jeer at poor Timmy! Didn't they realize how terribly uncomfortable a collar like that was – and Timmy had to wear it night and day! He couldn't even lie down comfortably. George mooned about looking so angry and miserable that her mother felt worried.

'George dear – don't be silly about this. You will make your father cross. Timmy will have to wear that collar for at least a week, you know – and he *does* look a bit comical when you first see him. He's getting used to it, he soon won't notice it.'

'Everybody laughs at him,' said George, in an angry voice. 'He went into the garden and a lot of kids hung over the wall and laughed like anything. And the postman told me it was cruel. And Father thinks it's funny. And . . .'

'Oh dear, George, don't get into one of your moods,' said her mother. 'Remember, Anne is coming soon. She won't enjoy things much if you behave like this.'

George bore it for one day more. Then, after two upsets with her father over Timmy, another with a couple of boys who laughed at him, and one with the paper-boy, she decided she wouldn't stay at Kirrin Cottage for one day longer!

'We'll take my little tent, and go off by ourselves somewhere,' she told Timmy. 'Some place where nobody can see you till your ear is better and that hateful collar is off. Don't you think that's a good idea, Timmy?'

'Woof,' said Timmy. He thought that any of George's ideas were good, though the collar puzzled him very much.

'You know the *dogs* laugh at you too, Timmy,' said George, earnestly. 'Did you see how that silly little poodle belonging to Mrs Janes up the lane stood and stared at you? He looked *exactly* as if he was laughing. I won't have you laughed at. I know you hate it.'

Timmy certainly didn't like it, but he really was not as upset about the collar as George seemed to be. He followed her as she went up to her bedroom and watched her as she began to put a few things into a small bag.

'We'll go to that lonely little spot on the common,' she said to him. 'We'll pitch our tent near a little stream, and we'll jolly well stay there till your ear's better. We'll go tonight. I'll take my bike, and strap everything on to the back.'

So, in the middle of the night, when Kirrin Cottage was dark and quiet, George stole downstairs with Timmy. She left a note on the dining-room table, and then went to get

her bicycle. She strapped her little tent on it, and the bag containing food and other odds and ends.

'Come on!' she whispered to the surprised Timmy. 'We'll go. I'll ride slowly and you can run beside me. Don't bark for goodness' sake!'

They disappeared into the darkness, Timmy running like a black shadow beside the bicycle. Nobody guessed they were gone. Kirrin Cottage was quiet and undisturbed – except for the creaking of the kitchen door, which George had forgotten to shut.

But in the morning, what a disturbance! Joan the cook found George's note first and wondered what a letter in

George's writing was doing on the dining-room table. She ran straight up to George's room and looked inside.

The bed was empty. There was no George and Timmy's basket was empty. Joan went to take the note to Mrs Kirrin.

'Oh *dear*! How silly George is!' she said, when she had read it. 'Look, Quentin – such a fuss about Timmy! Now George has gone off with him, goodness knows where!'

Her husband took the note and read it out loud. 'Dear Mother, I'm going off for a few days with Timmy till his ear is better. I've taken my tent and a few things. Don't worry, please. Tell Anne if she wants to join me, to come to the end of Carters Lane on the common and I will show her where I'm camping. Tell her to come at twelve. Love from George.'

'Well, I'm blessed!' said George's father. 'All right – let her stay away if she wants to – I'm tired of her sulky face and Timmy's hang-dog looks. Tell Anne to join George, and maybe I shall have peace for a few days!'

'George should be all right,' said his wife. 'She's quite sensible really – and she's got Timmy. I'll tell Anne to join her when she arrives this morning.'

When Anne arrived at Kirrin Station, and looked out for George and Timmy, they weren't there – only her aunt was there, smiling as usual.

'What's happened?' said Anne. 'Where's George – and Timmy?'

'Oh – George has gone off by herself,' said her Aunt Fanny. 'Come along, and I'll tell you!'

2

Anne Joins the Little Camp

Aunt Fanny soon told Anne about Timmy's ear and the big collar of cardboard that had caused all the trouble. Anne couldn't help smiling.

'Oh Aunt Fanny – George is quite crazy about old Tim, isn't she? I'll go and meet her at twelve, and of course I'll camp with her for a day or two. It's lovely weather and I'd like to. I expect Uncle Quentin will be glad to have us out of the house!'

'How are Julian and Dick?' asked her aunt. She was very fond of Anne's two brothers, George's cousins. 'Will they be coming down here at all these holidays?'

'I don't know,' said Anne. 'They're still in France, you know, on a school-boys' tour. I feel funny without them! George will be cross to hear they probably won't be coming to Kirrin. She'll just have to put up with *me*!'

At twelve o'clock Anne was standing patiently at the end of Carters Lane. It ran to the common and then ended in a small, winding path that led to nowhere in particular. Big gorse bushes grew here and there, and slender birch trees. Anne, her belongings strapped to her back, and a bag in her hand, looked over the common to see if she could spy George coming.

There was no sign of her. 'Blow!' said Anne. 'I suppose she's changed her mind or something. Perhaps her watch has stopped and she doesn't know the time. She ought to, though, by looking at the sun! How long shall I wait?'

She sat down by a big gorse-bush, out of the hot sun. She hadn't been there for more than a minute when she heard a hissing sound.

'Pssssst!'

Anne sat up at once. The sound came from the other side of the bush, and she got up and walked round it. Half-hidden under a prickly branch were George and Timmy!

'Hallo!' said Anne, surprised. 'Didn't you see me when I arrived? Hallo, Tim darling! How's your poor old ear? Oh, doesn't he look a quaint old dear in that collar, George?'

George scrambled out of the bush. 'I hid here just in case Father or Mother should come with you and try to make me come back,' she said. 'I wanted to make quite sure they weren't waiting somewhere a little way away. I'm glad you've come, Anne.'

'Of course I've come,' said Anne. 'I wouldn't stay alone at Kirrin Cottage while you were camping out. Besides, I understand how you feel about Timmy. The collar's a jolly good idea, of course – but it does make him look comical. I think he looks rather a dear in it, I do really.'

George was almost relieved that Anne had not laughed

at Timmy as most people had. She smiled at her cousin, and Timmy licked her till Anne really had to push him away.

'Let's go,' said George, scrambling up. 'I've got a lovely camping-place, Anne. You'll like it. It's near a little spring too, so there's plenty of water for Timmy to drink – and us too. Did you bring any more food? I didn't really bring much.'

'Yes. I've brought heaps,' said Anne. 'Aunt Fanny made me. She's not cross with you, George. I didn't see your father. He was shut up in his study.'

George's spirits suddenly rose. She gave Anne a friendly punch. 'This is going to be fun! Timmy's ear will soon be better, and he loves camping out as much as we do. I've really found a good place – about the loneliest on the common! Nobody near us for miles!'

They set off together, Timmy at their heels, darting off every now and again when he smelt rabbit.

'When are Julian and Dick coming down?' asked George. 'In a few days? Timmy's ear will be all right then and we can go back to Kirrin Cottage to welcome the boys, and have some fun there.'

'They may not be coming down at all these hols,' said Anne, and George's face fell at once. She stopped and stared at Anne in dismay.

'Not coming! But they *always* come in the hols – or we go away somewhere together!' she said. 'They *must* come! I shall be miserable without Ju and Dick.'

'Well – they're still in France, on a tour or something,' said Anne. 'We shall hear if they're staying on there or coming down to Kirrin, when we get back to the cottage. Don't look so woebegone, George!'

But George felt woebegone. The holidays stretched before her, suddenly seeming long and dreary. Her two boy cousins were always such fun – they had had such

16

wonderful adventures together. And now – now they weren't coming!

'We shan't have any adventures at all if the boys don't come,' she said, in a small voice.

'I shan't mind that,' said Anne. 'I'm the peaceful one, not always on the look-out for something to happen, like you and the boys! Perhaps these holidays will be quite unexciting without even the *smell* of an adventure! Oh George – cheer up! *Don't* look so mournful. You'd better send a telegram to Julian and Dick if you feel so badly about it.'

'I've a good mind to!' said George. 'I can't *imagine* hols without the boys. Why – we shan't be the Five – the Famous Five – if they don't come!'

'Woof!' said Timmy, quite agreeing. He sat down and tried to scratch his ear, but the big collar prevented him. He didn't seem to mind and ran off after a rabbit quite happily.

'I think *you* are more upset about that collar than Timmy,' said Anne, as they walked along. 'Are we getting near this place of yours, George? It's a jolly long way.'

'We go up this hill in front of us – and then drop down to a little copse,' said George. 'There's a funny old cottage nearby – quite ruined and empty. At first I thought perhaps people lived there, but when I went nearer I saw that it was ruined. There's a big old rose-rambler climbing all over it, even inside. I suppose the people who used to live there planted it.'

They walked up the little hill and down again, following curving rabbit-paths. 'Better look out for adders,' said Anne. 'This is just the kind of place for them. My word, it's hot, George. Is there anywhere to bathe near here – a pool or anything?'

'I don't know. We could explore and see,' said George. 'I did bring my swim-suit just in case. Look – you can see part of the old cottage now. My camp is fairly near there. I thought I'd better camp near the spring.'

They were soon at George's rough little camp. Her tent was up, and she had made a bed inside of the springy heather. A mug, a bag of dog biscuits, a few tins, and a loaf of bread were at one end of the tent. It didn't seem to Anne as if George had brought very much, and she felt glad that she had managed to pack such a lot of things.

'Aunt Fanny cut dozens and dozens of sandwiches,' said Anne. 'She said if we kept them in this tin they wouldn't go stale, and would last us a day or two till we went back. I'm hungry. Shall we have some now?'

They sat out in the sun, munching the ham sandwiches. Anne had brought tomatoes too, and they took a bite at a sandwich and then a bite at a tomato. Timmy had to make do with a handful of dog biscuits and half a sandwich every now and again. After a bit he got up and wandered off.

'Where's he going?' asked Anne. 'To look for a rabbit?'

'No. Probably to get a drink,' said George. 'The spring is in the direction he's gone. I'm thirsty too – let's take the mug and get a drink ourselves.'

They went off with the mug, Anne following George through the thick heather. The little spring was a lovely one. It had evidently been used by the people who had once lived in the old cottage, and was built round with big white stones, so that the spring ran through a little stony channel, as clear as crystal.

'Oooh – it's as cold as ice!' said Anne. 'Simply delicious! I could drink gallons of this!'

They lay on the heather out in the sun, talking, when they came back from the spring. Timmy wandered off by himself again.

'It's so peaceful here,' said Anne. 'Nobody near us for miles. Just the birds and the rabbits. This is what I like!'

'There's hardly a sound,' said George, yawning.

And then, just as she said that, there came a noise in the distance. A sharp sound, like metal on stone. It came again and again and then stopped.

'What's that, do you suppose?' said George, sitting up.

'I can't imagine,' said Anne. 'Anyway, it's a long way away – everything is so still that sounds carry from quite a distance.'

The sharp noises began again in a little while and then stopped. The girls shut their eyes, and slept. There wasn't a sound now except the pop-pop-pop of gorse pods exploding in the sun and sending out their little black seeds.

George woke up when Timmy came back. He sat down heavily on her feet and she woke up with a jump.

'Timmy! Don't!' she said. 'Get off my feet, you made me jump!' Timmy obligingly removed himself and then picked up something he had dropped, lay down and began gnawing it. George looked to see what it was.

'Timmy! That's a bone! Where did you get it?' she said. 'Anne, did you bring a bone for Tim?'

'What? What did you say?' said Anne, half asleep. 'A bone. No, I didn't. Why?'

'Because Timmy's found one,' said George, 'and it's a bone that has had cooked meat on it, so it's not a rabbit or anything Timmy's caught. Timmy, where did you get it?'

'Woof,' said Timmy, offering the bone to George, thinking that she too might like a gnaw, as she seemed so interested in it.

'Do you suppose anyone else is camping near us?' asked Anne, sitting up and yawning. 'After all, bones don't grow in the heather. That's quite a good meaty one, too. Timmy, have you stolen it from another dog?'

Timmy thumped his tail on the ground and went on with his bone. He looked pleased with himself.

'It's rather an old bone,' said George. 'It's smelly. Go away, Tim – take it further off.'

The sharp metallic noises suddenly began again and George frowned. 'I believe there *is* someone camping near us, Anne. Come on – let's do a bit of exploring and find out. I vote we move our camp if there are other people near. Come on, Timmy – that's right, bury that horrible bone! This way Anne!'

3

The Old Cottage – and a Surprise

The two girls, with Timmy at their heels, left their camping-place and set off in the hot sun. Anne caught sight of the ruined cottage and stopped.

'Let's have a look at it,' she said. 'It must be awfully old, George.'

They went in at the wide doorway. There was no door left, only the stone archway. Inside was a big room, whose floor had once been paved with slabs of white stone. Now grass and other weeds had grown between the cracks, and had actually lifted up some of the slabs so that the whole floor was uneven.

Here and there parts of the walls had fallen away and the daylight came through. One window was still more or less intact, but the others had fallen out. A small crooked stairway of stone led upwards in one corner.

'To rooms above, I suppose,' said Anne. 'Oh, here's

another doorway, leading into a second room – a small one. It's got an old sink in it, look – and this must be the remains of a pump.'

'There's not much to see, really,' said George, looking round. 'The top rooms must be quite ruined, because half the roof is off. Hallo, here's another door – a back door. It's actually a *door* too, not just a doorway.'

She gave a push at the stout wood – and the old door promptly fell off its hinges and crashed outwards into an over-grown yard.

'Goodness!' said George, startled. 'I didn't know it was quite so rotten. It made poor Tim jump almost out of his skin!'

'There are out-houses here – or the remains of them,' said Anne, exploring the back-yard. 'They must have kept pigs and hens and ducks. Here's a dried-up pond, look.'

Everything was falling to pieces. The best preserved corner of the old place was what must have been a small stable. Rusted mangers were still there and the floor was of stone. An old, old piece of harness hung on a big nail.

'It's got quite a nice "*feel*" about it, this old place,' said Anne. 'Sometimes I don't like the feel of places – they give me an uneasy feeling, a feeling that horrid things may have happened there. But this is quite different. I think people have been happy here, and led peaceful lives. I can almost hear hens clucking and ducks quacking, and pigs gr . . .'

'Quack, quack, quack! Quack!'

'*Cuck*-cuk-cuk-cuk-cuk! *Cuck*-cuk-cuk-cuk-cuk!'

Anne clutched George and the two girls looked extremely startled to hear the sudden loud noise of quacking and clucking. They stood and listened.

'What was it?' said Anne. 'It *sounded* like hens and ducks – though I'm not quite sure. But there aren't any here, surely. We shall hear a horse whinnying next!'

They didn't hear a whinny – but they heard the snorting of a horse at once. 'Hrrrrr-umph! Hrrrrr-umph!'

Both girls were now quite alarmed. They looked for Timmy. He was nowhere to be seen! Wherever could he have got to?

'*Cuck*-cuk-cuk-cuk-cuk!'

'This is silly,' said George. 'Are we imagining things? Anne, there *must* be hens near. Come round the back of these stables and look. Timmy, where are you? TIMMY!'

She whistled shrilly – and immediately an echo came – or so it seemed!

'Phee-phee-phee-phee-phee!'

'TIMMY!' yelled George, beginning to feel as if she was in a dream.

Timmy appeared, looking rather sheepish. He wagged his tail – and to the girls' enormous amazement, they saw that he had a ribbon tied on it. A ribbon – a bright blue one at that!

'Timmy! Your tail – the ribbon – Timmy, what's all this about?' said George, really startled.

Timmy went to her, still looking sheepish, and George tore the ribbon off his tail. 'Who tied it there?' she demanded. 'Who's here? Timmy, where have you been?'

The two girls searched the old buildings thoroughly, and found nothing and nobody. Not a hen, not a duck, not a pig – and certainly not a horse. Then – what was the explanation? They stared at one another in bewilderment.

'And where did Timmy get that silly ribbon?' said George, exasperated. '*Someone* must have tied it on.'

'Perhaps it was a hiker passing by – perhaps he heard us here and saw Timmy and played a joke,' said Anne. 'But it's strange that old Tim *let* him tie on the ribbon. I mean – Timmy's not overfriendly with strangers, is he?'

The girls gave up the idea of exploring any further and went back to their little camp. Timmy went with them. He lay down – and then suddenly got up again, making for a thick gorse bush. He tried to squirm underneath.

'*Now* what's he after?' said George. 'Really, I think Timmy's gone mad. Timmy, you *can't* get under there with that great collar on. TIMMY, do you hear me!'

Timmy backed out reluctantly, the collar all crooked. After him came a peculiar little mongrel dog with one blind eye and one exceedingly bright and lively one. He was half-white and half-black, and had a ridiculously long thin tail, which he waved about merrily.

'*Well*!' said George, amazed. 'What's that dog doing there? And how did Timmy get so friendly with him? Timmy, I can't make you out.'

'Woof,' said Timmy, and brought the mongrel dog over to Anne and George. He then proceeded to dig up the smelly bone he had buried, and actually offered it to the little dog, who looked away and took no interest in it at all.

'This is all very peculiar,' said Anne. 'I shall expect to see Timmy bring a cat to us next!'

At once there came a pathetic mewing.

'Mee-ew! Mee-ew-ee-ew-ee-ew!'

Both dogs pricked up their ears, and rushed to the bush. Timmy was once again kept back by his big collar and barked furiously.

George got up and marched to the bush. 'If there's a cat there, it won't have much chance against two dogs,' she called to Anne. 'Come away, Tim. Hey, you little dog, come away, too.'

Timmy backed out, and George pulled out the small dog very firmly indeed. 'Hold him, Anne!' she called. 'He's quite friendly. He won't bite. I'm going to find that cat.'

Anne held on to the small mongrel, who gazed at her excitedly with his one good eye and wagged his tail violently. He was a most friendly little fellow. George began to crawl into the bare hollow space under the big gorse bush.

She looked into it, not able to see anything at first, because it was dark there after the bright sunlight. Then she got a tremendous shock.

A round, grinning face stared back at her, a face with very bright eyes and tousled hair falling on to the forehead. The mouth was set in a wide smile, showing very white teeth.

'Mee-ew-ee-ew-ee-ew!' said the face.

George scrambled back at top speed, her heart thumping. 'What is it?' called Anne.

'There's somebody hiding there,' said George. 'Not a cat. A fathead of a boy who is doing the mewing.'

'Mew-ee-ew-ee-ew!'

'Come out!' called Anne. 'Come out and let's see you. You must be crazy.'

There was a scrambling noise and a boy came head-foremost from the hollow space under the bush. He was about twelve or thirteen, short, sturdily built, and with the cheekiest face Anne had ever seen.

Timmy rushed at him and licked him lovingly. George stared in amazement.

'How does my dog know you?' she demanded.

'Well, he came growling at me yesterday when I was in my own camp,' said the boy. 'And I offered him a nice meaty bone. Then he saw my little dog Jet – short for jet-propelled, you know – and made friends with him – and with me too.'

'I see,' said George, still not at all friendly. 'Well, I don't like my dog to take food from strangers.'

'Oh, I couldn't agree more,' said the boy. 'But I thought I'd rather he ate the bone than ate *me*. He's a nice dog, yours. He feels a bit of an idiot wearing that collar, doesn't he? You should have heard Jet laugh when he first saw it!'

George frowned. 'I came here to be alone so that Timmy shouldn't be jeered at,' she said. 'He's got a bad ear. I suppose *you* were the fathead who tied a blue ribbon on his tail?'

'Just for a joke,' said the boy. '*You* like frowning and glaring, I can see. Well, *I* like joking and tricking! Your Timmy didn't mind a bit. He took to my dog right away. But everyone likes Jet! I wanted to find out who owned Timmy – because, like you, *I* don't like strangers messing about when I'm camping out. So I came along.'

'I see. And you did all the clucking and quacking and hrrr-umphing?' said Anne. She liked this idiot of a boy, with his broad friendly grin. 'What are you doing – just camping – or hiking – or botanizing?'

'I'm digging,' said the boy. 'My father's an archaeologist – he loves old buildings more than anything else in the world. I take after him, I suppose. There was once an old Roman camp on this common, you know – and I've found a place where part of it must have been, so I'm digging for anything I can find – pottery, weapons, anything like that. See, I found this yesterday – look at the date on it!'

He suddenly thrust an old coin at them – a queer, uneven one, rather heavy to hold.

'It's date is 292,' he said. 'At least, as far as I can make out. So the camp's pretty old, isn't it?'

'We'll come and see it,' said Anne, excited.

'No, don't,' said the boy. 'I don't like people messing round me when I'm doing something serious. Please don't come. I won't bother you again. I promise.'

'All right. We won't come,' said Anne, quite understanding. 'But don't you play any more silly tricks on us, see?'

'I promise,' said the boy. 'I tell you, I won't come near you again. I only wanted to see whose dog this was. Well, I'm off. So long!'

And, whistling to Jet, he set off at a furious pace. George turned to Anne.

'What a peculiar boy!' she said. 'Actually – I'd rather *like* to see him again. Wouldn't you?'

4

That Night

It was now tea-time, according to Anne's watch and also according to everyone's feelings, including Timmy's. Timmy felt the heat very much and was always wandering off to the little spring to lap the crystal-cold water. Anne wished that she and George had a big jug that they could fill – it was such a nuisance to have to keep running to and fro with just a mug.

They had tea – biscuits, a sandwich each, and a bar of rather soft chocolate. George examined Timmy's ear for the hundredth time that day, and pronounced it very much better.

'Well, don't take off that collar yet,' said Anne. 'He'll only open the wound by scratching if you do.'

'I'm not *going* to take it off!' said George, touchily. 'What shall we do now, Anne? Go for a walk?'

'Yes,' said Anne. 'Listen – you can hear those sharp, metallic noises again – that's the boy at work again, I expect. Funny boy he must be – coming to dig about all on his own with his comical little dog. I wish we could see what he's doing.'

'We promised we wouldn't,' said George. 'So I don't feel that we even ought to go and peep.'

'Of course not!' said Anne. 'Come on – let's go in the opposite direction, George – right away from the boy. I hope we shan't get lost!'

'Not while Timmy's with us, silly!' said George. 'You'd find your way home from the moon, wouldn't you, Tim?'

'Woof,' agreed Timmy.

'He always says yes to whatever you say, George,' said Anne. 'I say – isn't it a lovely evening? I wonder what Julian and Dick are doing?'

George immediately looked downcast. She felt that her two cousins had no right to go rushing across France when she wanted them at Kirrin. Didn't they like Kirrin? Would they be having magnificent adventures on the Continent, and not want to spend even a week at Kirrin? She looked so lost in miserable thoughts that Anne laughed at her.

'Cheer up! At least *I* am here with you – though I agree that compared with Ju and Dick I'm very poor company, and not at all adventurous!'

They had a lovely walk, and sat down half-way to watch hordes of rabbits playing together. Timmy was very unhappy about this. Why *sit down* to watch silly rabbits? Rabbits were made to *chase*, weren't they? Why did George always put a restraining hand on his collar when she sat down to watch rabbits? He whined continually, as he watched with her.

'Shut up, Timmy, you ass,' said George. 'You'd only spoil the entertainment if you sent them to their holes.'

They watched for a long while and then got up to go back to the camp. When they came near, they heard the sound of low whistling. Someone was about that evening, quite near their camp. Who was it?

They came round a big gorse bush, and almost bumped into a boy. He got out of their way politely, but said nothing.

'Why – it's *you*!' said George, in surprise. 'I don't know your name. What are you doing here? You said you wouldn't come near us.'

The boy stared, looking very surprised. His tousled hair fell right across his forehead, and he brushed it back.

'I said nothing of the sort,' he said.

'Oh, you *did*!' said Anne. 'You know you did. Well, if you break your promise, there's no reason for us to keep ours. We shall come and visit *your* camp.'

'I never made you any promise,' said the boy, looking quite startled. 'You're mad!'

'Don't be an idiot,' said George, getting cross. 'I suppose you'll be saying next that you didn't act like a hen, and a duck, and a horse this afternoon . . .'

'And a cat,' said Anne.

'Barmy!' said the boy, looking at them pityingly. 'Quite barmy.'

'Are you coming here again?' demanded George.

'If I want to,' said the boy. 'The water in this spring is better than the one over by my camp.'

'Then we shall come and explore *your* camp,' said George, firmly. 'If you don't keep your promise, we shan't keep ours.'

'By all means come if you want to,' said the boy. 'You seem quite mad, but I daresay you're harmless. But don't bring your dog. He might eat mine.'

'You know he wouldn't eat Jet!' said Anne. 'They're good friends.'

'I don't know anything of the sort,' said the boy, and went off, brushing his hair out of his eyes again.

30

'What do you make of *that*?' said George, staring after him. 'Not a bit the same as he was this afternoon. Do you think he really *had* forgotten about his promise and every-thing?'

'I don't know,' said Anne, puzzled. 'He was so perky and jolly and full of fun before – grinning all the time – but just now he seemed quite serious – not a smile in him!'

'Oh well – perhaps he's a bit crazy,' said George. 'Are you sleepy, Anne? I am, though I can't think why!'

'Not very – but I'd like to lie down on this springy heather and watch the stars gradually come sparkling into the sky,' said Anne. 'I don't think I'll sleep in the tent, George. You'll want Timmy with you, and honestly there's so little room inside the tent that I'm quite sure Timmy would lie on my legs all night long.'

'I'll sleep in the open air as well,' said George. 'I only slept in the tent last night because it looked a bit like rain. Let's get some more heather and make a kind of mattress of it. We can put a rug on top of it, and lie on that.'

The two of them pulled a lot of heather and carried it to their 'bed'. Soon they had a fine pile, and Timmy went to lie on it.

'Hey – it's not for you!' cried George. 'Get off – you'll flatten it right down. Where's the rug, Anne?'

They laid the rug on the heather-pile and then went to the spring to wash and clean their teeth. Timmy im-mediately got on to the heather-bed again, and shut his eyes.

'You old fraud!' said George, lugging him off. 'You're not asleep. Keep off our bed! Look – there's a nice soft patch of grass for you. That's your bed!'

George lay down on the rug, and the heathery-bed sank a little beneath her weight. 'Very comfortable!' said George. 'Shall we want a rug over us, Anne?'

'Well, I did bring one,' said Anne. 'But I don't think we'll want it, the night's so hot. Look – there is a star already!'

Soon there were six or seven – and then gradually hundreds more pricked through the evening sky as the twilight deepened. It was a wonderful night.

'Don't the stars look big and bright?' said Anne, sleepily. 'They make me feel very small, they're such millions of miles away. George, are you asleep?'

There was no answer. George hadn't heard a word. She was fast asleep. Her hand fell down the side of the heather and rested on the ground below. Timmy moved a little nearer and gave it a small lick. Then he too fell asleep, and gave some small doggy snores.

The night darkened. There was no moon but the stars shone out well from the midnight sky. It was very quiet out there on the common, far away from streets and villages and towns. Not even an owl hooted.

Anne didn't quite know why she awoke. At first she had no idea where she was, and she lay gazing up at the stars in astonishment, thinking she must still be asleep.

She suddenly felt very thirsty. She groped about in the nearby tent for the mug, couldn't find it and gave it up.

'I'll drink from my cupped hands,' she thought, and set off for the little spring. Timmy wondered whether to follow her. No – he would stay with George. She wouldn't like it if she awoke and found him gone with Anne. So he settled his head down on his paws again and slept, leaving one ear open for Anne.

Anne found the little spring. Its tinkling gurgling sound guided her as soon as she heard it. She sat down on one of the stones nearby, and held out her cupped hands. How very cold the water was – and how delicious to drink on this hot night! She sipped thirstily, slopping some of the water down her front.

She got up to go back, and walked a few steps in the
starlight. Then she stopped. Wait – was she going in the
right direction? She wasn't sure.

'I *think* I am!' she decided, and went on, carefully and
quietly. Surely she must be near their little camp now?

Then all at once she stood still, and felt herself stiffen.
She had suddenly seen a light. It had flashed and disappeared. Ah – there it was again! Whatever could it be?

Then, as her eyes strained through the starlit darkness, she suddenly saw that she *had* taken the wrong way – she had gone in the direction of the old ruined cottage, and not the camp – and the light had come from there!

She didn't dare go any nearer. She felt glued to the grass she was standing on! Now she could hear sounds – whispering sounds – and the noise of a footfall on the stone floor of the cottage – and then the flash of a light came again! Yes, it *was* from the old cottage!

Anne began to breathe fast. Who was it in the old cottage? She simply dared not go and see. She must go back to George, and to Timmy's protection. As fast and as silently as she could she found her way back to the spring – and then, almost stumbling now, made her way to where George was still lying peacefully asleep.

'Woof,' said Timmy, sleepily, and tried to lick her hand. Anne climbed on to the heathery-bed beside George, her heart still beating fast.

'George!' she whispered. 'George, do wake up. I've something queer to tell you!'

5

That Boy Again!

George would not wake up. She grunted when Anne poked her and prodded her, and then she turned over, almost falling off the small heather-bed.

'Oh George – *please* do wake!' begged Anne, in a whisper. She was afraid of speaking out loud in case anyone should hear her. Who knew what might happen if she drew attention to their little camp?

George awoke at last and was cross. 'Whatever is it, Anne?' she said, her voice sounding loud in the night.

'Sh!' said Anne. 'Sh!'

'Why? We're all alone here! We can make as much noise as we like!' said George, surprised.

'George, do listen! There's someone in that old cottage!' said Anne, and at last George heard and understood. She sat up at once.

Anne told her the whole story – though it didn't really seem very much of a tale when she related it. George spoke to Timmy.

'Tim!' she said, keeping her voice low. 'We'll go and do a little exploring, shall we? Come on, then – and keep quiet!'

She slid off the rug and stood up. 'You stay here, she said to Anne. 'Timmy and I will be very quiet and careful, and see what we can find out.'

'Oh no – I couldn't stay here *alone*!' said Anne in alarm, and got up hurriedly. 'I shall have to come too. I don't mind a bit now Timmy's with us. I wonder he didn't bark at the people in the old cottage, whoever they were.'

'He probably thought it was you messing about,' said George, and Anne nodded. Yes, of course, Timmy must have thought that any noises he heard had been made by her.

They took the path that led to the old cottage. George had Timmy well to heel. He knew he must not push forward unless told to. His ears were pricked now, and he was listening hard.

They came cautiously to the cottage. They could see its dark outline in the starlight, but little else. There was no light flashing there. Nor did there seem to be any noises at all.

All three stood still and quiet for about five minutes. Then Timmy moved restlessly. This was boring! Why wouldn't George let him run forward and explore every-where if she wanted to know if intruders were about?

'I don't think there's a soul here!' whispered George into Anne's ear. 'They must have gone – unless you dreamed it all, Anne!'

'I didn't!' whispered back Anne indignantly. 'Let's go forward a bit and send Timmy into the cottage. He'll soon bark if there's anyone there.'

George gave Timmy a little shove. 'Go on, then!' she said. 'Find, Timmy, find!'

Timmy gladly shot forward into the darkness. He

trotted into the cottage, though it was impossible even to see him go to it. The two girls stood and listened, their heart-beats sounding very loud to them! There was not a sound to be heard, except occasionally the rattle of Timmy's strong claws on a stony slab.

'There can't be anyone there,' said George at last, 'else Timmy would have sniffed them out. You're an ass, Anne – you dreamt it all!'

'I did not!' said Anne, indignant again. 'I *know* there was someone there – in fact, more than one person, because I'm sure I heard whispering!'

George raised her voice. 'Timmy!' she called loudly, making Anne jump violently. 'Timmy! Come along. We've sent you on a silly wild goose chase – but now we'll go back to bed!'

Timmy came trotting out of the cottage and went obediently to George. She heard him yawn as he stood beside her, and she laughed.

'Anne had a bad dream, that's all, Timmy,' she said.

Anne felt cross – very cross. She said no more and they left the old cottage and went back to their heather-bed. Anne climbed on to her side and turned over with her back to George. All right – let George think it was a dream if she liked!

But when Anne awoke in the morning and remembered the happenings of the night before, she too began to wonder uneasily if she *had* dreamed what she had seen and heard in the old cottage.

'After all – Timmy would certainly have caught anyone who was there,' she thought. 'And he wasn't at all excited, so there can't have *been* anyone in the cottage. And anyway, why would they come? It's just silly!'

So, when George talked about Anne's dreaming in the middle of the night, Anne did not defend herself. She really could *not* be sure that it had really happened. So she held her tongue when George teased her, and said nothing.

'Let's go and see that boy and his camp,' George said when they had eaten a few rather stale sandwiches and some shortbread biscuits. 'I'm beginning to feel bored, aren't you? I wish Timmy's ear would quite heal up. I'd go back home like a shot then.'

They set off in the direction of the camp with Timmy. They heard a chip-chipping noise as they came near, and then something small and hairy shot out from a bush and rushed up, barking a welcome.

'Hallo, Jet!' said Anne. 'Don't you let Timmy have any more of your bones!'

The chipping noise had stopped. The two girls went on and came to a very messy piece of common. It had been well dug over, in some places very deeply. Surely that boy couldn't have done so much excavating by himself?

'Hey! Where are you?' called George. Then she saw the boy below her, examining something in a trench he had dug out. He jumped and looked upwards.

Then he scowled. 'Look – you promised not to come and disturb me!' he shouted. 'You're mean. Just like girls to break a promise.'

'Well! I like *that*!' said George, amazed. 'It was *you* who broke yours! Who came messing round *our* camp yesterday evening I'd like to know?'

'Not me!' said the boy at once. 'I always keep my promises. Now go away and keep yours. Girls! Pooh!'

'Well, I can't say we think much of *you*,' said George, disgusted. 'We're going. *We* don't want to see anything of your silly digging. Good-bye!'

'Good-bye and good riddance!' called the boy rudely, and turned back to his work.

'I think he must be *quite* mad,' said Anne. 'First he makes a promise – then last evening he broke his promise and even said he hadn't made one – and now today he says he *did* make a promise and that he'd kept his and we'd broken ours. Idiotic!'

They went up a little rabbit path, and into a small copse of birch trees. Someone was sitting there reading. He looked up as they came.

The two girls stopped in amazement. It was that boy *again*! But how had he got here? They had just left him behind in a trench! Anne looked at the title of the book he was reading. Goodness – what a learned title – something about Archaeology.

'Another little trick of yours, I suppose?' said George, sarcastically, stopping in front of him. 'You must be a jolly good runner, I must say, to have got here so quickly. Funny boy, aren't you – very very funny!'

'Good gracious – it's those potty girls again,' groaned the boy. 'Can't you leave me alone? You talked a lot of rubbish yesterday – and now you're talking it again.'

'How did you get here so quickly,' said Anne, puzzled.

'I didn't get here quickly. I came very slowly, reading my book as I went,' said the boy.

'Fibber!' said George. 'You must have run at top speed. Why do you pretend like this? It's only a minute or so ago that we saw you.'

'Now *you're* the fibber!' said the boy. 'I do think you two girls are awful. Go away and leave me alone and never let me see you again!'

Timmy didn't like the tone of the boy's voice and he growled. The boy scowled at him. 'And just you shut up too,' he said.

Anne pulled at George's sleeve. 'Come on,' she said, 'it's no good staying here arguing. The boy's crazy – mad – we'll never get any sense out of him!'

The two girls walked off together, Timmy following. The boy took absolutely no notice. His face was turned to his book and he was quite absorbed in it.

'I've never met anyone *quite* so mad before!' said Anne, rather puzzled. 'By the way, George – you don't suppose it could have been that idiotic boy last night in the cottage?'

'No. I tell you I think you dreamed it,' said George, firmly. 'Though that boy is quite idiot enough to explore an old cottage in the middle of the night. He would probably think it a very good time to do so. Oh Anne, look – there's a pool – in that hollow there. Do you think we could bathe in it?'

It certainly shone very temptingly. They went down to have a closer look. 'Yes – we'll have a swim this after-noon,' said George. 'And then I really think, Anne, we ought to go back to Kirrin Cottage and get a few more provisions. The sandwiches we've got left are so dry that we really shan't enjoy eating them – and as Timmy's ear isn't healed, it looks as if we'll have to stay a bit longer.'

'Right!' said Anne, and they went on back to the camp. They changed into their swim-suits in the afternoon and went off to the little pool. It was fairly deep, very warm and quite clean. They spent a lovely hour swimming and basking and swimming again – then they reluctantly dressed and began to think of going off on the long journey to Kirrin Cottage.

George's mother was very surprised to see the two girls and Timmy. She said yes, of course they could have some more food, and sent them to ask Joan for all she could spare.

'By the way, I've heard from Julian and Dick,' she said. 'They're back from France – and may be here in a day or two! Shall I tell them to join you or will you come back here?'

'Tell them to come and fetch us as soon as they get here!' said George, delighted. Her face shone. Ah – the Five would be together again. How wonderful!

'Leave me directions to give them so that they can find you,' said her mother. 'Then you can all come back – together. The boys can help to carry everything.'

41

What fun, what fun! Julian and Dick again, now things would be exciting, things would happen, as they always did. What FUN!

6

Storm in the Night

It was fun to go back to their little camping-place again. It was growing dark, as they had stayed to have a good meal at Kirrin Cottage, and Timmy had eaten a most enormous plate of meat, vegetables and gravy. Then he had sat down and sighed as if to say 'That was jolly good! I could do with some more!'

However, nobody took any notice of this, so he trotted off to have a good look round the garden to make sure it was just the same as when he had left it a day or two before. Then it was time to start back to the camping-place, and Timmy heard George's whistle.

'Well, nobody laughed at Timmy this evening!' said Anne. 'Not even your father!'

'Oh, I expect Mother had told him not to,' said George. 'Anyway, I *said* I would stay away till Tim's ear is better, and I mean to.'

'Well, I'm quite willing,' said Anne. 'The only thing

I'm a bit worried about is – do you suppose there will be anyone snooping about in that old cottage again?'

'You dreamed it all!' said George. 'You admitted you did!'

'Well, yes, I did wonder if I *had* dreamed it,' said Anne, as they walked up the long Carters Lane to the moor. 'But now that it will soon be dark, I'm beginning to think I *didn't* dream it – and it isn't a very nice feeling.'

'Oh, don't be silly!' said George impatiently. 'You can't chop and change about like that. Anyway, we've got Timmy – no one would dare to upset Timmy! Would they, Tim?'

But Timmy was ahead, hoping against hope that he might for once in a while catch a rabbit. There were so many about on the common at this time of the evening, peeping at him here, making fun of him there, and showing their little white bobtails as soon as he moved in their direction.

The two girls got safely back to their camp. The tent was still up, their heather-bed out in the open, covered with the old rug. They put down their loads thankfully, and went to the little spring for a drink.

George yawned. 'I'm tired. Let's get to bed at once, shall we? Or wait – perhaps it would be a good idea to have a look in at that cottage to make sure no one is there to disturb us tonight.'

'Oh no – I don't want to look,' said Anne. 'It's getting dark now.'

'All right – I'll go with Timmy,' said George, and off she went. She came back in about five minutes, her little torch shining in front of her, for it was now almost dark.

'Nothing to report,' she said. 'Nothing whatever – except one bat flying round that big room. Timmy nearly went mad when it flew down and almost touched his nose.'

44

'Oh. That's when he barked, I suppose,' said Anne, who was now curled up on the heather-bed. 'I heard him. Come on, George – I'm sleepy.'

'I must just look at Timmy's ear once more,' said George and shone her torch on it.

'Well, buck up, then,' said Anne. 'That's about the thousandth time today you've examined it.'

'It does seem much better,' said George, and she patted Timmy. 'I *shall* be glad when I can take this awful collar off him. I'm sure he hates it.'

'I don't believe he even *notices* it now,' said Anne. 'George, are you coming or not? I really can't keep awake one minute more.'

'I'm coming,' said George. 'No, Tim – you are *not* sleeping on our bed. I told you that last night. There's hardly enough room for Anne and me.'

She climbed carefully on to the heather-bed, and lay looking up at the twinkling stars. 'I feel happy tonight,' she said, 'because Julian and Dick are coming. I was down in the dumps when I thought they might not be coming at all these hols. When do you suppose they'll be here, Anne?'

There was no answer. Anne was asleep. George sighed. She would have liked to plan what they were going to do when the boys came. Timmy's ear would surely be all right in a day or two – and the boys could carry everything back from this little camp to Kirrin Cottage – and then long days of swimming and boating and fishing and all kinds of fun could begin – begin – begin – be . . .

And now George was asleep too! She didn't feel a small spider running over her hand, wondering whether or not to spin a web between her finger and thumb. She didn't hear the scramble of a hedgehog not far off – though Timmy did and pricked one ear. It was a very peaceful night indeed.

Next day the girls were very cheerful. They made a good breakfast of some of the food they had brought, and then spent some time getting more heather for their bed, which, under the weight of their two bodies, was now rather flat and uncomfortable.

'Now for a swim!' said George. They put on their swim-suits, threw cardigans over their shoulders and set off to the little pool. On the way they saw Jet, the little mongrel dog, in the distance, and the boy with him. Jet tore up to them and danced round Timmy excitedly.

The boy called to them. 'It's all right, don't worry, I'm not going near your place! I'm still keeping *my* promise! Jet – come here!'

The girls took no notice of the grinning boy, but couldn't resist patting the little one-eyed mongrel. Jet really was like a piece of quicksilver, darting in and out and round about. He shot back to the boy at once.

The girls went on to the pool – and stopped in dismay when they came near. Someone was already there, swimming vigorously!

'Who is it?' said Anne. 'Dear me, this lonely common seems absolutely *crowded* with people!'

George was staring at the swimmer in utmost amazement. 'Anne – it's that boy!' she said. 'Look – tousled hair and everything! But – but . . .'

'But we've just met him going in the opposite direction!' said Anne, also amazed. 'How extraordinary! No, it *can't* be the boy!'

They went a little nearer. Yes – it *was* the boy. He called out to them. 'I'm just going out. I shan't be a minute!'

'How did you get here?' shouted George. 'We never saw you turn back and run.'

'I've been here for about ten minutes,' shouted back the boy.

'Fibber!' yelled back George at once.

'Ah – barmy as usual!' yelled the boy. 'Same as yester-day!'

He got out and walked off, dripping wet, in the direction of the trenches and pits which he was digging. George looked about for Jet, but she couldn't see him. 'Perhaps he's in the pool too,' she said. 'Come on, Anne – let's swim. I must say that that boy is extraordinary! I suppose he thinks it's funny to meet people, then double back and appear again!'

'He was nicer the first time of all that we saw him,' said Anne. 'I liked him then. I just don't understand him now. Ooooh – isn't this water lovely and warm!'

They had a long swim, got out and basked in the sun, lying on the heather, and then swam again. Then they began to feel hungry and went back to their little camping place.

The day passed quickly. They saw no more of the puzzling boy, or of Jet. They occasionally heard the sharp noise of metal on stone, or of chipping, from the place where the boy was presumably still digging in the old Roman camp.

'Or what he *hopes* is an old Roman camp,' said George. 'Personally I think he's so mad that I don't suppose he would know the difference between a Roman camp and a Boy Scouts' camp!'

They settled down on their heather-bed that night but saw no stars twinkling above them this time. Instead there were rather heavy clouds, and it was not nearly so warm.

'Gosh – I hope it's not going to rain!' said George. 'Our tent wouldn't be much good against a real downpour! We could squeeze into it all right, but it's not a proper waterproof tent. Do you think it's going to rain, Anne?'

'No,' said Anne, sleepily. 'Anyway, I'm not getting up till I have to! I'm tired.'

She went to sleep, and so did George. Timmy didn't,

though. He had heard the far-off growl of thunder, and he was uneasy. Timmy was not afraid of thunderstorms, but he didn't like them. They were things that growled like enormous dogs in the sky, and flashed angrily – but he never could get at them, or frighten them!

He closed both eyes, and put down one ear, leaving the other one up, listening.

Another thunder growl came, and one large and heavy drop of rain fell on Timmy's black nose. Then another fell on his cardboard collar and made a very loud noise indeed, startling him. He sat up, growling.

The rain came closer, and soon large drops, the size of ten-penny pieces, peppered the faces of the two sleeping girls. Then came such a crash of thunder that they both awoke in a fright.

'Blow! It's a thunderstorm!' said George. 'And thunder rain too. We shall be soaked.'

'Better get into the tent,' said Anne, as a flash of lightning forked down the sky and lighted up everything with a quick brilliance.

'No good,' said George. 'It's soaked already. There's nothing for it but to get into the cottage, Anne. At least we'll have a roof over our heads or rather, a ceiling, for the roof's gone. Come on.'

Anne didn't in the least want to shelter in the old cottage, but there was absolutely nothing else to do. The girls grabbed their rug and ran through the rain, George flashing her torch to guide them. Timmy ran too, barking.

They came to the doorway of the cottage and went inside. What a relief to get out of the rain! The two girls huddled down into a corner, the rug round them – but soon they were too hot and threw it off.

The storm passed overhead with a few terrific crashes and much lightning. Gradually the rain grew less and

soon stopped. One star came out, and then others followed as the thunder-clouds swept away in the wind.

'We can't go back to the tent – we'll have to stay here,'
said George. 'I'll go and get our bags for pillows. We can
lie on the rug.'

Anne went with her, and carried a bag back too. Soon

the girls were lying in a corner of the rug, their heads on the bags, and Timmy close beside them.

'Good night,' said Anne. 'We'll try to go to sleep again! Blow that storm!'

Soon they were both asleep – but Timmy wasn't. Timmy was uneasy. Very uneasy! And quite suddenly he broke into a volley of such loud barks that both girls woke up in a panic.

'Timmy! What's the matter? Oh Tim, what is it?' cried George. She clutched his leather collar and held on to him.

'Don't leave us! Timmy, what's scared you?'

7

Queer Happenings

Timmy stopped barking and tried to get away from George's hand on his collar. But she would not let him. George was not easily frightened, but what with the thunderstorm, the queer old cottage and now Timmy's sudden excitement, she wanted him near her.

'What is it?' asked Anne, in a scared whisper.

'I don't know. I can't even imagine,' said George, also in a low voice. 'Perhaps it's nothing – just the thunderstorm that has upset him and made him nervous. We'll keep awake a bit, and see if we hear anything queer.'

They lay quietly in their corner, and George kept a firm hand on Timmy. He growled once or twice, but did not bark any more. George began to think it really must have been the storm that had upset him.

A rumble of thunder came again – the storm was returning, or else another one was blowing up!

George felt relieved. 'It's all right, Anne. It must have

been the thunder and lightning in the distance that upset Timmy. You're silly, Timmy – scaring us like that!'

Crash – rumble – crash! Yes, certainly the storm was gathering force again! Timmy barked angrily.

'Be quiet! You make more noise than the thunder!' said George, crossly. 'No you can't go out into the rain, Timmy. It's begun again, as bad as before. You'd only get dripping wet – and then you'd want to come and sit as close to me as possible and make me wet too. I know you!'

'No – don't let him go, George,' said Anne. 'I like him here with us. My word – what a storm! I hope it won't strike this cottage.'

'Well, considering that it must have stood here for three or four hundred years, and have seen thousands of storms, I expect it will come safely through one more!' said George. 'Where are you going, Anne?'

'Just to look out of the window,' said Anne. 'Or out of the place where the window used to be! I like to see the countryside suddenly lit up for just one moment in a lightning flash – and then go back to darkness again.'

She went to stand at the window. There came the crash of thunder, not far away, and a brilliant flash of lightning. Anne stared over the countryside, which had suddenly become visible in the flash – and then disappeared like magic in a second!

Anne gave a sudden cry and stumbled back to George. 'George – George . . .'

'Whatever's the matter?' asked George, alarmed.

'There's someone out there – people!' said Anne, clutching George and making her jump. 'I saw them just for an instant, when the lightning flashed.'

'People? What sort of people?' said George, astonished. 'How many?'

'I don't know. It was all so quick. I think there were

two – or maybe three. They were standing some way off – quite still, out there in the storm.'

'Anne, those are *trees*!' said George, scornfully. 'There are two or three small trees standing against the sky out there – I noticed them the other day.'

'These weren't trees,' said Anne. 'I know they weren't. What are people doing out there in this storm? I'm frightened.'

George was absolutely certain that Anne had seen the group of little trees that she knew were there – they would look just like people, in a quick flash of lightning. No sooner did you see something in a storm than it was gone!

She comforted Anne. 'Don't worry, Anne! It's the easiest thing in the world to imagine seeing things in a lightning flash. Timmy would bark if there were people around. He would . . .'

'Well, he *did* bark, didn't he?' said Anne. 'He woke us both up with his barking.'

'Ah yes – but that was just because he heard the storm coming up again,' said George. 'And you know he gets angry when he hears the thunder growling.'

Just at that moment the thunder crashed again – then the lightning flashed its weird and brilliant light.

This time *both* the girls screamed, and Timmy gave an enormous bark, trying his hardest to get away from George.

'There! Did you see *that*?' said Anne, in a shaky voice.

'Yes. Yes, I did. Oh, Anne, you're right! Someone was looking in at the window! And if we saw him, he must have seen *us*! Whatever is he doing here in the middle of the night?'

'Well, I told you I saw two or three people,' said Anne, still shakily. 'I expect it was one of them. Maybe they saw the cottage in one of the lightning flashes, and thought

they might shelter here – and sent one of their number to see.'

'Maybe. But what in the world is anyone *doing*, wandering about here at night?' said George. 'They can't possibly be up to any good. Let's go home tomorrow, Anne. I wish the boys were here! They'd know what to do, they would have some good plan!'

'The storm's going off again,' said Anne. 'Timmy has

stopped barking too, thank goodness. Don't let him go, George. You never know – those people, whoever they are, might do him harm. Anyway, I feel safer when he's with us!'

'I wouldn't dream of letting him go,' said George. 'You're trembling, Anne! You needn't be as scared as that! Timmy won't let you come to any harm.'

'I know! But it wasn't very nice suddenly seeing some-body looking in at the window like that, outlined in a lightning flash!' said Anne. 'I can't possibly go to sleep again. Let's play some silly game to take our minds off it.'

So they played the Alphabet game with Animals. Each had to think in turn of an animal beginning with A, and a mark went to the one who could keep it up longest! Then they went on to B and to C and to D.

They were doing the E's when they heard a loud and very comforting sound.

'Timmy's snoring,' said George. 'He's fast asleep. What an elephantine snore, Tim!'

'E for elephant,' said Anne, quickly.

'Cheat! That should have been *my* E!' said George. 'All right. E for Eland.'

'E for Egg-Eater,' said Anne, after a pause.

'Not allowed – you made that up!' said George. 'My mark!'

By the time they got to M, Anne was two marks ahead, and the dawn was breaking. It was a great relief to the two girls to see the silvering of the sky in the east and to know that soon the sun would be up. They immediately felt much better. George even stood up and went bravely to the window, where there was nothing to be seen but the quiet countryside outside, with its stretches of heather, gorse-bushes and silver birches.

'We were silly to be so scared,' said George. 'I don't think we'll go back home today after all, Anne. I hate running away from anything. The boys would laugh at us.'

'I don't care if they do,' said Anne. 'I'm going back. If the boys were here, I'd stay – but goodness knows when they'll come – it might not be till next week! I'm just NOT staying here another night.'

'All right, all right,' said George. 'Do as you like – but for goodness' sake tell the boys it was *you* who wanted to run away, not me!'

'I will,' said Anne. 'Oh dear – now I feel sleepy all over again. I suppose it's because daylight is here and everything seems safe, so I know I can fall asleep.'

George felt the same! They cuddled down together on the rug again and immediately fell asleep. They did not wake till quite late – and even then something woke them, or they might have slept on for hours, tired out with their broken night and the fright they had had.

They were awakened by something scuttling round them, making a very loud noise indeed. Then Timmy barked.

The girls awoke and sat up, rather dazed. 'Oh, it's *Jet*!' said Anne. 'Jet, have you come to see if we're all right, you dear, funny little one-eyed thing!'

'Wuff-wuff!' said Jet and rolled over on his back to be tickled, his long thin tail wagging all the time. Timmy leaped on him and pretended to eat him. Then a loud voice called to them.

They looked up. The boy was standing at the door, grinning widely.

'Hallo, sleepy-heads! I came to see if you were all right after that awful storm. I know I promised I wouldn't come here, but I felt a bit worried about you.'

'Oh. Well, that's nice of you,' said Anne, getting up and brushing the dust from her skirt. 'We're quite all right – but we had rather a queer night. We . . .'

She got a hard nudge from George and stopped suddenly. George was warning her not to say anything about the people they had seen – or the person at the window. Did she think they might have anything to do with this boy? Anne said no more and George spoke instead.

'Wasn't it a dreadful storm? How did you get on?'

'All right. I sleep down in a trench, and the rain can't get at me. Well – so long! Come on, Jet!'

The boy and the dog disappeared. 'That was nice of him,' said Anne. 'He doesn't seem crazy this morning, does he – quite normal! He didn't even contradict us. I think I quite like him after all.'

They went to their soaked tent and got a tin of sardines out to eat with bread and butter. Just as they were opening it, they heard someone whistling and looked up.

'Here comes that boy again!' said Anne.

'Good morning. I don't want to butt in – but I just wondered if you were all right after the storm,' said the boy, without even a smile. The girls stared at him in amazement.

'Look – don't start being crazy all over again!' said George. 'You know jolly well we're all right. We've already told you.'

'You haven't. And I *didn't* know!' said the boy. 'Well, I only came out of politeness. Sorry to see you are still barmy!'

And off he went. 'There!' said Anne, vexed. 'Just as we thought he was nice again, and not crazy, he starts all over again. I suppose he thinks it's funny. Silly ass!'

They set their things out to dry in the sun, and it was half-past twelve before they were ready to pack and go back to Kirrin Cottage. George was rather cross about going, but Anne was quite firm. She was NOT going to spend another night on the common.

George was just strapping a package on her bicycle,

when the two girls heard the sound of voices – and then Timmy went quite mad! He barked wildly, and set off down a path at top speed, his tail wagging nineteen to the dozen!

'Oh! It can't be – surely it can't be Julian and Dick!' shouted George, in sudden delight, and she shot off after Timmy.

It was! It *was* Julian and Dick! There they came, packs on their backs, grinning all over their faces! Hurrah! The Famous Five were all together once more!

8

All Together Again!

There was such excitement at the arrival of the boys that at first nobody could make themselves heard. Timmy barked at the top of his very loud voice and simply would *not* stop! George shouted, and Dick and Julian laughed. Anne hugged them, and felt proud of two such brown, good-looking brothers.

'Ju! We never guessed you'd come so soon!' said the delighted George. 'Gosh, I'm pleased to see you!'

'We got fed up with French food,' said Dick. 'I came out in spots and Julian was sick, and it was SO hot. Phew! Next time I go there I'll go when it's cooler.'

'And we kept on thinking of Kirrin and the bay, and you two girls and Timmy,' said Julian, giving George a friendly punch. 'I think we *really* got a bit homesick. So we packed up before we should, and flew home.'

'Flew?' said George. 'You lucky things! And then did you come straight down here?'

'We spent the night with Mother and Dad at home,'

said Julian, 'and then caught the first train here that we possibly could this morning – only to find that you weren't at Kirrin!'

'So we packed camping-out things in smaller bags and came straight along to you!' said Dick. 'I say, George, old thing, do you think you could possibly make Timmy stop barking? I'm going a bit deaf!'

'Shut up, Tim,' ordered George. 'Let other people bark a bit. Do you notice his collar, Julian?'

'Can't help seeing it!' said Julian. 'He looks a scream in it, doesn't he? Ha ha! You're an Elizabethan dog with a ruff, Timmy – that's what Uncle Quentin told us – and that's what you look like, old fellow!'

'He looks most comical, I must say,' said Dick. 'Enough to make a cat laugh, hey, Timmy!'

Anne looked at George. Goodness, what would she say to hear *Julian and Dick* laughing at Timmy and making fun of him! Would she lose her temper at once?

But George only grinned. In fact she gave a little laugh herself. 'Yes – he does look funny, doesn't he? But he doesn't mind a bit!'

'You know, we came here to camp because George couldn't bear people laughing at . . .' began Anne, thinking that she wouldn't let George get away with this! But George gave her such a beseeching look, that she stopped at once. George could never bear to look small in front of Julian and Dick. She prided herself on being just like a boy – and she was suddenly certain that her two cousins would think she was 'just like a *girl*' if they heard of the fuss she had made about people laughing at Timmy's collar.

'I say – you two seem to be packing up,' said Julian, looking at the package strapped to the back of George's bicycle. 'What's happened?'

'Well – it got a bit lonely and Anne was . . .' and then in her turn George caught a beseeching look from Anne! She knew what it meant. 'I didn't tell tales of *you* – so don't tell tales of *me* – *don't* say I was scared!'

'Er – Anne was certain that there was something queer going on here,' went on George, who had quite meant to say that Anne was scared and insisted on going home. 'And we didn't feel that we could tackle it ourselves – though if you had been here we wouldn't have *dreamed* of going home, of course.'

'What do you mean – something queer?' asked Dick.

'Well – you see – it began like this,' said George, but Julian interrupted.

'If there's a tale to tell, let's have it over a meal, shall we? We've had nothing to eat since six o'clock this morning, Dick and I – and we're ravenous!'

'Yes. Good idea,' said Dick, and began to undo a big package which he took out of his bag. 'I've a picnic lunch here from your mother, George – a jolly good one, I can tell you. I think she was so relieved to think that she was going to get rid of us that she really surpassed herself! We've got a marvellous piece of boiled ham – look! It'll last us for ages – if we don't give bits to Timmy. Get away, Tim. This is *not* for you! Grrrrrr!'

George suddenly felt so happy that she could hardly speak. It had been fun camping with Anne – but what a difference the boys made! So confident of themselves, so merry, full of jokes, so idiotic, and yet so dependable. She felt that she wanted to sing at the top of her voice!

The sun had been hot again that morning and had dried the common beautifully. It wasn't long before the Five were sitting down in the heather with a very fine feast before them.

'I wouldn't sell anyone my hunger for a hundred pounds,' said Dick. 'Now then – who's going to carve this magnificent piece of gammon?'

There were no plates, so they had to make sandwiches

of the ham. Dick had actually brought some mustard, and dabbed it generously over the slices of ham before George put them between pieces of bread. 'Aha, Tim – this is one way of making sure you won't get even a *bite* of these wonderful ham sandwiches!' said Dick. 'You can't bear mustard, can you? Ju, where's the meat we brought for Tim?'

'Here. Pooh – it smells a bit strong,' said Julian. 'Do you mind taking it to a nice secluded corner, Tim?'

Timmy immediately sat down close to Julian. 'Now –

don't be so disobedient!' said Julian, and gave Timmy a friendly push.

'He doesn't understand the word "secluded",' said George, with a grin. 'Tim – buzz off a bit!'

Timmy understood that and took his meat a little way away. Everyone took a ripe red tomato, and a little lettuce heart from a damp cloth brought by Julian, and settled down happily to munch sandwiches.

'Lovely!' said Anne, contentedly. 'Goodness gracious – I can hardly believe we had such a peculiar time last night!'

'Ah – tell us all about it!' said Dick.

So first Anne, then George related all that had happened. Anne told of the night she had seen a light in the old cottage and had heard whispers and footfalls inside.

'We did think I might have been dreaming,' she said, 'but now we don't think I was. We think I really did see and hear those things.'

'What next?' asked Julian, taking his third sandwich. 'This all sounds most interesting. Quite Famous Five-ish, in fact!'

George told of the storm in the night, and how they had had to leave their heather-bed and go to shelter in the old cottage – and how, in the flashes of lightning, Anne had seen two or three people standing outside – and then how they had *both* seen someone standing silently, looking in at the window.

'Queer,' said Julian, puzzled. 'Yes – something is up. I wonder what? I mean – there's absolutely nothing on this lonely bit of common that's at all interesting.'

'Well – there are the remains of an old Roman camp,' said Anne. 'And a boy there who is examining them to see if he can find anything old and interesting.'

'A completely *mad* boy,' said George. 'He doesn't seem to know what he says or doesn't say. Contradicts himself all the time – or to put it another way, tells the most idiotic fibs.'

'And he apparently thinks it's awfully funny to meet us somewhere, and then double round on his tracks and appear suddenly somewhere else,' said Anne. 'Sometimes I can't help liking him – other times he's too fat-headed for words.'

'He's got a little one-eyed dog called Jet,' said George, and Timmy gave a sudden bark as he heard the name. 'You like Jet, don't you, Tim?'

'This all sounds most interesting,' said Dick. 'Pass me the tomato bag, Ju, before you eat the lot. Thanks. As I said, *most* interesting – a one-eyed dog, a mad boy, Roman remains – and people who come to an old ruined cottage in the dead of night and look into windows!'

'I wonder you two girls didn't pack up and go home,' said Julian. 'You must be braver without us than I thought possible!'

George caught Anne's eye and grinned mischievously, but said nothing. Anne owned up, red in the face.

'Well – I did tell George I was going home this very morning, I was so scared last night. George didn't want to, of course, but she was coming, all the same. But now you've turned up, things are different.'

'Ah – well, do we stay on, or don't we, Ju?' said Dick. 'Are we scared or are we not?'

Everyone laughed. 'Well – if you go back *I* shall stay on alone!' said Anne. 'Just to show you!'

'Good old Anne!' said Dick. 'We all stay, of course. It may be nothing – it may be something – we can't tell. But we'll certainly find out. And the first thing to do is to have a look at the Roman remains and the mad boy. I'm looking forward to meeting him, I must say! After that we'll tackle the ruined cottage!'

Timmy came up to see if he could get any tit-bits. Julian

64

waved him away. 'You smell of too-strong meat, Timmy,' he said. 'Go and get a drink. By the way, *is* there anything to drink here, George?'

'Oh yes,' said George. 'A lovely spring. Not far off, either. Let's take the remains of our meal there, and the mug. We've only got one unfortunately, so it's no good getting water unless we all sit by the spring and take turns at the mug. Come on!'

The boys thought that the spring was a really splendid one. They grouped themselves around it and took turns at filling the mug and drinking from it. They were now eating slabs of Joan's fruit-cake and it was very good.

'Now, you girls unpack again,' said Dick, when they had finished their meal. 'Goodness, I did enjoy that! We'd better unpack too, Julian.'

'Right. Where shall we put our things?' asked Julian, looking around. 'I don't somehow like to leave everything under that little tent, with a mad boy about, and a one-eyed dog. I feel that both of them might like the rest of that ham.'

'Oh, it's too hot to leave ham out in this sun,' said George. 'We'll have to put it into the old cottage, on a shelf. We'll put *everything* there, shall we? Move in properly, in case it rains again at night. It's so tiresome to have to bundle everything indoors in the dark and the rain.'

'I agree,' said Dick. 'Right. We'll move into the ruined cottage. What fun! Come on, everyone!'

They spent the next half-hour taking their things into the cottage and putting them in corners or on shelves. George found a dark corner behind the fireplace where she put the food, for she was half-afraid that Jet, nice little dog though he seemed, might perhaps smell the ham and gobble up most of their food.

'Now!' said Julian, 'are we ready to go and see the

Roman remains and the Mad Boy? Here we go, then – the Famous Five are off again, and who knows what will happen!'

9

A Little Exploration

The Five walked off together, Timmy at the back, delighted to have all his friends with him again. He kept nudging first one person's heels and then another, just to remind them that he was there.

As they came near the old camp, they saw a boy sitting beside a bush, reading.

'There's that boy we told you of!' said George. 'See?'

'He looks fairly ordinary,' said Dick. 'Very absorbed in his book, I must say. Determined to take no notice of us!'

'I'll speak to him,' said George. So, as they drew near, she called to the boy.

'Hallo! Where's Jet?'

The boy looked up, annoyed. 'How do I know?'

'Well, he was with you this morning,' said George.

'He was not,' said the boy. 'He's never with me! Please don't disturb me, I'm reading.'

'There you are!' said George to the others. 'He came to

see us this morning with Jet – and now he says the little dog is never with him. Quite, quite mad!'

'Or plain rude,' said Dick. 'Not worth bothering about, anyway. Well, if he's not doing any excavating in his Roman Camp, perhaps we can explore it without being ordered off!'

They walked on slowly and came to the camp, and at once heard a cheerful whistling going on, and the sound of someone digging. George looked over the top of the dug-out trench in surprise. She almost toppled in, she was so amazed at what she saw!

The boy was there, digging carefully, whistling as he did so! He brushed his tousled hair from his hot forehead and caught sight of George and the others. He looked rather astonished.

'How on earth did you get down here so quickly?' said George. 'Do you have wings or something?'

'I've been down here all the afternoon,' said the boy. 'For at least an hour, I should think.'

'Fibber!' said George. The boy looked very angry, and shouted back at once.

'I'm tired of you two girls – and now you've brought your friends too, I suppose you think you can come and aggravate me even more!'

'Don't be a fathead,' said Dick, feeling as puzzled about this boy as George and Anne had been. How in the world had be run around them and got down in the trench so quickly? Did he enjoy playing tricks like that? He really didn't *look* mad!

'Is this your property, this old camp?' asked Julian.

'No. Of course not. Don't be daft!' said the boy. 'As if I could own a whole camp like this! It was discovered by my father some time ago, and he gave me permission to work here for the hols. It's pretty exciting, I can tell you. See my finds?'

He pointed to a rough shelf where stood a broken pot, something that looked like an old brooch, a long pinlike thing, and part of a stone head. Julian was at once interested. He leapt down into the trench.

'I say – you've certainly got something there!' he said. 'Any coins too?'

'Yes – three,' said the boy and put his hand in his

pocket. 'I found this one first – then these two close together yesterday. They must be hundreds and hundreds of years old.'

By this time all the others were down in the trench too. They looked about with much interest. Evidently the place had been well excavated by experts, and now the boy was working here and there on his own, hoping to find something that had been overlooked.

Dick went out of the trench and began to clamber about over the great stones and rocks. A small animal suddenly caught his eye – a young rabbit.

It stared at him in fright and then disappeared behind a slab of stone. It peeped out at Dick again, and he was amused. He went cautiously over to the slab, and the little rabbit disappeared – but soon two or three whiskers poked out. Dick got down on hands and knees and looked behind the slab. A dark hole was there.

Dick pulled out his torch and flashed it into the hole, wondering if the small rabbit was hiding there, or whether it was the entrance to a burrow.

To his surprise there was a very big hole indeed – a hole that seemed to go down and down and down – his torch could make out no bottom to it.

'It's far too wide for a rabbit-hole,' thought Dick. 'I wonder where it leads to. I'll ask that boy.'

He went back to where the boy was still showing his things to Julian, talking eagerly. 'I say,' began Dick, 'there's a most interesting hole behind one of the stone slabs over there – what is it?'

'Oh that – my father says it was explored and that it was only a place for storage – meat in hot weather, or loot, or something like that. Actually nothing whatever was found there – most uninteresting. As a matter of fact it may be nothing to do with the Camp at all.'

'I say, look – here's another shelf with things on it,' said

George, suddenly spying a little collection of things on a rough shelf in another part of the trench. 'Are these yours too?'

'Those? No,' said the boy. 'Nothing to do with me at all. Don't touch them, please.'

'Whose are they then?' asked George, curiously. The boy took no notice whatever of her question and went on talking to Julian. George took down a beautiful little round pot.

'Hey! I told you NOT to touch those!' yelled the boy, so suddenly and angrily that George almost dropped the pot. 'Put it back – and clear out if you can't do what you're told.'

'Easy, old man, easy!' said Julian. 'No need to yell at her like that. You scared that little dog of yours and made him jump almost out of his skin! We'd better go, I think.'

'Well – I don't like being disturbed too much,' said the boy. 'People always seem to be wandering around. I've turned off quite a lot.'

'People?' said Julian, remembering Anne's story of two or three figures standing outside the cottage the night before, and of someone looking in. 'What kind of people?'

'Oh – nosey ones – wanting to get down and explore – disturbing me – it's surprising how many idiots there are wandering about this lonely place,' said the boy, picking up a tool again and setting to work. He grinned suddenly. 'I don't mean you. You really *know* something about this kind of thing.'

'Was anyone about last night?' asked Julian.

'Well – I rather think so,' said the boy. 'Because Jet here barked like mad. But it might have been the storm that frightened him – not that he's *usually* frightened of storms.'

'What's your name?' asked Dick.

'Guy Lawdler,' said the boy, and Dick whistled.

'My word – is your father the famous explorer, Sir John Lawdler?' he asked. The boy nodded.

'Well, no wonder you're so keen on archaeology!' said Dick. 'Your father's done pretty well in that line, hasn't he?'

'Come on, Dick!' said George. 'Let's go now. We might have time for a swim in the pool. We forgot to tell you about that.'

'Right,' said Dick. 'Come on, Julian. Good-bye, Guy!'

They left the rather desolate old camp and went back to the cottage to get their swim-suits and change. It wasn't long before they were running over the heather to the pool.

'Hallo – Guy's having a swim!' said Dick, in surprise. Sure enough, a boy was there, his hair falling over his forehead as usual.

'Hey, Guy!' shouted George. 'Have a swim with us!'

But the boy was already getting out of the water. Dick shouted. 'Wait a minute – don't go. We'd like to have a swim with you, Guy!'

But the boy turned defiantly. 'Don't be an ass!' he said. 'My name's not Guy!'

And, leaving four astonished people behind him, he ran lightly over the heather and disappeared.

'There you are – he's mad after all!' said Anne. 'Don't bother about him. Come on in – the water's lovely and warm.'

They lazed about afterwards and began to feel hungry. 'Though how *any* of us could feel hungry after eating about fifty sandwiches between us at dinner-time, I don't know!' said Dick. 'Race you back to the cottage, Ju!'

They changed back into ordinary clothes and then had tea – fruit cake, shortbread biscuits and tinned pineapple on bread. They kept the juice and diluted it with cold spring water – it was simply delicious.

'Now let's explore the cottage,' said Dick.

'We already have, Anne and I,' said George. 'So I don't expect you'll find anything much.'

They went methodically through the old house, and even up the old stone stairway to the two rooms upstairs – though they could hardly be called rooms, for they had very little roof and not much wall!

'Nothing much here, that's certain,' said Dick, clattering down the stone stairway. 'Now let's go to the outbuildings – not that there's much left of them either!'

They examined everything, and came last of all to the old stables. It was dark inside, for the windows were very small, and it was some seconds before anyone could see properly.

'Old mangers,' said Dick, touching them. 'I wonder how long ago it is since they were used – and . . .'

'I say!' said George, suddenly. 'There's something funny here. Anne, look – this bit of floor was undisturbed yesterday, wasn't it?'

Anne looked down at the big white flagstone on which George was standing. It was quite obvious that it had been lifted, for the edges were not as green with moss as the others were, and the stone had been put back a little crookedly.

'Yes – someone's been interested in this stone – or in what is beneath it!' said Dick. 'I bet something is buried underneath!'

'Those men last night – that's what they came about!' said George. 'They went into these stables and lifted this stone. Why?'

'We'll soon find out!' said Julian. 'Come on, everyone, loosen it with your fingers – then we'll heave it up!'

10

What Can Be Happening?

Forty fingers and thumbs were very hard at work trying to loosen the heavy stone. At last Julian got hold of a corner which could be held more easily than any other part of the stone. He tried to lift it and it came away a little.

'Help me this side, Dick,' said Julian, and Dick put his strong fingers there too. 'Heave-ho!' he said – and up came the stone.

It went over with a crash and Timmy barked loudly, jumping aside. Everyone peered down – and then looked exceedingly disappointed!

There was nothing there at all. Not even a hole! The black earth, hard as iron, lay underneath, and nothing else.

They all stared down at the dry, hard earth, puzzled. George looked up at Julian.

'Well – that's queer, isn't it? Why should anyone lift up this heavy stone if there is nothing hidden underneath?'

'Well, it's clear that whoever was here didn't find anything – nor did he *hide* anything either,' said Julian. 'Dear me – why should anyone lift up a heavy stone and put it back – just for nothing?'

'He was obviously looking for something that wasn't here,' said Anne. 'The wrong stone, probably!'

'Yes. I think Anne's right,' said Dick. 'It's the wrong stone! Probably there is something very interesting under the *right* stone! But which one is it?'

They all sat and looked at one another, and Timmy saw it too, wondering why all this fuss was made about a flat white stone. Julian thought hard.

'From what you've told me, Anne – about seeing a light in the cottage that first night you were here – and hearing voices – and then seeing those figures outside last night in the storm – it looks as if someone is urgently hunting for something round about here.'

'Yes – something under a stone. Treasure of some sort, do you think?' said George.

Julian shook his head. 'No. I hardly think that much treasure would be hidden anywhere about this old cottage – all the people who lived here must have been fairly poor. The most they would have hidden would have been a few pieces of gold, and that would have been found long ago.'

'Well – someone modern might have hidden something valuable here – even something stolen,' said Anne.

'Yes. We can't tell. It's obviously important and urgent to somebody,' said Dick. 'I wonder if the people that Guy said came bothering him were anything to do with this?'

'They may have been,' said Julian. 'But they have

clearly decided that what they are looking for is here now, whatever it is. And they must have been most annoyed to find you and Anne here last night, George. That's why someone came and looked in at the window, I expect – to make sure you were asleep! And you weren't.'

'I don't know whether I want to stay on here or not now,' said Anne, alarmed. 'If they haven't found what they want, they'll probably come again – in the night too.'

'Who cares?' said Dick. 'We've got Timmy, haven't we? I'm not turning out of here because somebody's got a habit of turning up big stones!'

Julian laughed. 'Nor am I. Let's stay on! And I don't see why we shouldn't do a bit of pulling up of stones ourselves! We might come across something very interesting!'

'Right. It's decided that we stay on then, is it?' said Dick. 'What about you, Anne?'

'Oh yes – of course I'll stay,' said Anne, not wanting to in the least, but knowing that she simply could not bear not to be with the others.

The Five walked round and about the cottage for a while, trying to make out where the people that the girls had seen the night before had come from – from what direction did they come and where did they go?

'The figures I saw first in the lightning stood about there,' said Anne, pointing. 'Let's go and see if there are any foot-prints. It was pouring with rain and the ground must have been very muddy.'

'Good idea,' said Dick, and off they went to where Anne had pointed. But it was a heathery piece of ground, and difficult to tell even if anyone *had* trodden there, for the heather was thick and springy.

'Let's look just outside the window now – the one where Anne saw someone looking in,' said Dick. And there they had a find! Just in front of the window were two quite deeply-printed foot-marks. One was slightly blurred as if the maker of them had turned his foot sideways as he waited. The other was very clear indeed.

Dick got out a piece of paper. 'I rather think I'll measure these,' he said, 'and make a note of the pattern on the soles. They had rubber soles and heels – look at the markings – crêpe rubber I should think.'

He measured the prints. 'Size eight shoes,' he said. 'Same as yours, Ju.' Then he carefully drew an exact picture of the sole and heel markings.

'You're quite a detective, Dick,' said Anne, admiringly, and he laughed.

'Oh, anyone can copy foot-prints!' he said. 'The thing is to match them up with the owner!'

'I have a feeling it's getting on for supper-time – if anyone *wants* any supper,' said George. 'It's half-past eight! Would you believe that the time could fly so fast?'

'I don't *really* feel very hungry,' said Dick. 'We've done pretty well today.'

'Well, don't waste our precious food if you don't feel hungry,' said George. 'We shall have to keep going home for more if we eat everything too quickly.'

Nobody felt terribly hungry. They made a cosy corner in the cottage and had a slice of cake and a biscuit each, with a drink of pineapple juice and spring-water. George had had the bright idea of filling the big empty pine-apple tin, and they each filled a mug from it in turn, and drank.

'It's getting dark,' said Julian. 'Are we going to sleep inside the cottage or out?'

'In,' said Dick, promptly. 'We'll make things just as difficult for any night-prowlers as possible!'

'Right,' said Julian. 'I bet they won't be pleased to find old Timmy here too. Shall we go out and get some heather for beds? I don't fancy sharing a thin rug between the four of us.'

Soon they were all dragging in armfuls of the springy heather. They laid it in the front room, in two corners, for the boys thought they would rather be in the same room as the girls, in case of danger.

'You need an awful lot of heather to make a *soft* bed,' said Dick, trying his. 'My bones seem to go right through the clumps and rub against the floor!'

'We can put our anoraks over our heather,' said Julian. 'That will help. The girls can have the rug. We shan't need any covering, it's so hot.'

By the time they had finished, it was dark. George lay on her heather and yawned. 'I'm going to sleep,' she announced. 'We don't need to keep guard or anything like that, do we? Timmy will bark if anyone comes near.'

'You're right. I really don't think we need take turns at keeping awake,' said Julian. 'Move up, Dick – you've left me no room.'

Julian was the last to go to sleep. He lay awake puzzling over the lifted stone slab. It was clear that someone had expected to find something under it. How did they know it was that particular slab? Had they a map? If so, it must have shown the wrong stone – or perhaps the searchers read the map wrong?

Before he could work it out any further, he was asleep. Timmy was asleep too, happy because all the others were under his care. He had one ear open as usual, but not *very* much open!

It was enough to let him hear a small mouse of some kind run across the floor. It was even enough for him to hear a beetle scraping its way up the wall. After a while his ear dropped down and he didn't even hear a hedgehog outside.

But something caused his ear to listen again and it

pricked up. A noise crept inside the cottage – a noise that got louder and louder – a weird and puzzling noise!

Timmy woke up and listened. He pawed at George, not knowing whether to bark or not. He knew he should not bark at owls, but this was not an owl. Perhaps George would know.

'Don't, Timmy,' said George sleepily, but Timmy went on pawing her. Then she too heard the noise and sat up in a hurry.

What a truly horrible sound! It was a whining and a wailing, rising and falling through the night. A sound of misery and woe, that went on and on.

'Julian! Dick! Wake up!' called George, her heart beating wildly. 'Something's happening.'

The boys awoke at once and so did Anne. They sat and listened to the weird noise. What in the world could it be? There it went again – wailing high in the air, and then dying away with a moan, only to begin again a few seconds later.

Dick felt the roots of his hair pricking. He leapt off the heather-bed and ran to the window. 'Quick! Come and look at this!' he cried. 'What is it?'

They all crowded to the window, Timmy barking now as loudly as he could. In silence the others gazed at a very strange sight.

Blue and green lights were shining here and there, sometimes dimly, sometimes brightly. A curious round white light was travelling slowly in the air, and Anne clutched George, breathing fast.

'It won't come here,' she said. 'It won't, will it? I don't like it. What is happening, Julian?'

'I wish that awful wailing, whining noise would stop,' said Dick. 'It gets right inside my head. Do you make anything of all this, Julian?'

'Something's queer abroad,' said Julian. 'I'll go out

with Timmy and see what I can find.' And before anyone could stop him, out he went, Timmy barking beside him.

'Oh Julian – come back!' called Anne, listening as his footsteps became distant. They all waited tensely at the window – and then suddenly the wailing noise stopped and the strange lights gradually began to fade.

Then they heard Julian's footsteps coming back firmly in the darkness.

'Ju! What was it?' called Dick, as his brother came in at the doorway.

'I don't know, Dick,' said Julian, sounding very puzzled. 'I simply – don't – know! Perhaps we can find out in the morning.'

11

Interesting
Discoveries – and a Plan

The four sat in the dark and talked over the horrible noises and the weird blue and green and white lights. Anne sat close to Julian. She really was frightened.

'I want to go back to Kirrin,' she said. 'Let's go tomorrow. I don't like this.'

'I didn't see a thing just now,' said Julian, puzzled, his arm close round Anne. 'I seemed to go quite close to those wailing sounds – and then they stopped as soon as I got fairly near. But although Timmy barked and ran around, there didn't seem to be anyone there.'

'Did you get near the lights?' asked Dick.

'Yes, fairly near. But the odd thing was that they seemed high up when I got near them – not near the ground as I expected. And *again* Timmy couldn't find anyone. You would have thought if there was anyone

82

about, playing the fool, that Timmy would have found them. But he didn't.'

'Woof,' said Timmy, dolefully. He didn't like this queer business at all!

'Well, if *nobody's* making the noises and lights, it makes it even worse,' said Anne. 'Do let's go home, Julian. To-morrow.'

'All right,' said Julian. 'I don't feel particularly thrilled about all this myself. But there is *one* idea I've got in my mind which I'd like to sort out tomorrow.'

'What's that?' said Dick.

'Well – it may quite well be that somebody very badly wants us out of here for some reason,' said Julian. 'And that somebody may want to come and lift other stones and have a thorough search all over the place – which he can't do with us around. So he's trying to frighten us out!'

'Yes – I believe you are right, Julian,' said Dick. 'Those noises – and lights – they would be enough to scare any-one out of a place. Too eerie for words! Well – let's have a good snoop round in the daylight, to see if we can find any trace of a trickster!'

'We will – but it's extremely odd that *Timmy* didn't find him,' said Julian. 'Timmy can smell anyone out of any hiding-place! Yes – we'll have a very very good hunt round tomorrow.'

'And if you find nothing and nobody, we'll go home?' asked Anne.

'Yes, we will. I promise you,' said Julian, hugging Anne. 'Don't worry. You shan't have to stay here one night longer, unless you want to! Now – let's try and go to sleep again!'

It took the four a long time to go to sleep after all this excitement in the middle of the night. Anne kept listening for the wailing noises again, but none came. She kept her eyes shut tightly in case she should happen to see any more of the queer lights outside the window.

George and the boys lay awake too, puzzling out the problems of lights and noises which were not apparently caused by anyone! Julian especially was puzzled.

Only Timmy was unconcerned. He went to sleep before anyone else, though he kept one ear *wide* open – and up went the other one when George moved, or Dick whispered to Julian.

The excitement of the night made them all sleep late. Julian awoke first, and stared at the low ceiling in surprise. Now – where was he? In France? No. Ah, of course he was in the old ruined cottage!

He woke Dick, who yawned and stretched. 'Remember those queer lights and noises last night?' asked Dick. 'What a fright they gave us! It seems silly to think we were all so puzzled and scared, now that the sun is shining in at the window, and we can see the countryside around for miles!'

'I'm pretty certain someone is trying to scare us away,' said Julian. 'We are in their way here – they want to do some thorough explorations and they can't, because of us! I've a good mind to take the girls home, Dick, and come back here with you.'

'Anne might go, but George wouldn't,' said Dick. 'You know what old George is – good as any boy, and as full of courage as any boy, too. Let's not decide anything till we have had a look round this morning. I don't really believe there's anything spooky about this at all – I agree with you that it's just a few tricks to frighten us away.'

'Right,' said Julian. 'Let's wake the girls. Hey, George! Anne! Sleepyheads! Get up and get us breakfast! What are girls for if not to get our meals?'

George sat up, looking furious, as Julian intended. 'You

jolly well get your own m . . .' she began, and then laughed as she saw Julian's amused face.

'I was only just striking a little match to set you alight!' said Julian. 'Come on – let's all go for a swim in the pool!'

They set off together happily in the warm sunshine, Timmy padding along, his tail waving vigorously. As soon as they got to the pool, they saw the boy there, floating lazily on his back.

'There's Guy!' said Anne.

'I wonder if he will admit to his name or not this morning!' said George. 'Remember how he told us his name was Guy – and then said it wasn't a little while after? Silly ass! I can't make out if he's quite mad, or just thinks it's funny to keep playing the fool!'

They came to the pool. The boy waved to them, grinning. 'Come on in – it's fine!'

'Is your name Guy this morning or not?' called George.

The boy looked surprised. 'Of course it's Guy!' he said. 'Don't be idiotic! Come on in and have a game.'

They had a fine swim and a mad one. Guy was like an eel, swimming under the water, catching their legs, splashing, swimming away fast, doubling round and going underwater just as they got up to him!

At last they all sat panting on the edge of the pond, the sun shining down warmly on them.

'I say, Guy – did you hear anything strange last night?' asked Dick. 'Or see anything?'

'I didn't *see* anything strange – but I thought I heard somebody wailing and crying in the distance,' said Guy. 'Just now and again when the wind brought the sound this way. Jet didn't like it at all – did you, Jet? He went and hid under my legs!'

'We heard it too – quite near us,' said Julian. 'And saw strange lights.'

They discussed the matter for some time, but Guy could

not really help them, because he had not been near enough to the noises to hear them as clearly as the others had.

'I'm getting hungry,' said George, at last. 'I keep thinking of ham and tomatoes and cheese. Let's go back to the cottage.'

'Right,' said Julian. 'Good-bye, Guy – see you some-time soon. Good-bye, Jet, you mad little thing.'

They went off together, their swim-suits almost dry already in the sun.

'Well, Guy was perfectly sensible this morning,' said Anne. 'Funny! I wonder why he's so silly sometimes.'

'See – isn't that him – running down the path there – to the right, look!' said George, suddenly. 'Now how did he get there so quickly? We left him by the pool!'

It certainly looked like Guy! They called to him, but he didn't even look round or wave, though he must have heard them. They went on, puzzled. How could one person be so different each time – and why? What was the point?

They had a good breakfast and then went out to look round and see if they could find anything to explain the strange happenings of the night before.

'The noises seemed to come from about here, when I came out last night,' said Julian, stopping near the little group of trees. 'And the lights seemed to start about here too – but not near the ground – they were high up, above my head.'

'Above your head?' said Dick, puzzled. 'That seems odd.'

'It doesn't!' said Anne. 'Not a *bit* odd! What about those trees there? Couldn't somebody climb up them and do the wailing and whining there, with some strange instru-ment – and set off the weird lights?'

Julian stared up at the trees and then round at Anne. He grinned suddenly.

'Anne's got it! Clever girl! Of course someone was up there – or maybe two people – one doing the noises with some weird instrument and the other playing about with fireworks of some kind. Not the noisy kind – just coloured fire or balloons lighted up from inside.'

'Yes! *That's* why the lights seemed to be so high up,

when you came out!' said Dick. 'They were sent out by someone up in a tree!'

'And floated away to scare us,' said Anne. 'Golly – I *do* feel glad that it was silly tricks like that that frightened us so. They wouldn't frighten me *again*!'

'It explains something else too,' said George. 'It explains why Timmy didn't find anyone! They were safely up trees! I bet they hardly breathed when they knew Tim was down below.'

'Yes. Of course! That puzzled me too,' said Julian. 'It was too spooky for words when even old Tim couldn't find anyone real about – just noises and lights!'

'Here's something, look – a wrinkled little rubberskin – pale green!' said Dick, picking something up from the ground. 'That's what those lights were – balloons lighted up from inside in some way and sent floating away in the air.'

'Most ingenious,' said Julian. 'I expect they had quite a lot of funny tricks at their disposal last night. Yes – they certainly mean to scare us away!'

'Well, they won't,' said Anne, unexpectedly. '*I'm* not going, for one. I won't be scared away by stupid tricks!'

'Good old Anne!' said Julian, and clapped her on the back. 'Right – we'll all stay – but I've got an idea.'

'What?' asked everyone.

'We'll *pretend* to go!' said Julian. 'We'll pack up everything – remove our things from here – and go and camp somewhere else. But Dick and I will *hide* somewhere here tonight – and watch to see if anyone comes, and where they look for whatever it is they're hunting for, and why!'

'That's a wizard plan,' said Dick, pleased. 'We'll do it! Roll on, tonight! Adventure is about – and we'll be ready for it!'

12

A Good Hiding-Place

The Five spent quite a pleasant day, but when late afternoon came, they decided that it was time to carry out their plan and pack as if they were leaving.

'I imagine someone is spying on our doings,' said Dick. 'And won't he be pleased to see us apparently on the point of leaving!'

'How can anyone be spying?' asked Anne, looking all round as if she expected to see someone behind a bush. 'Timmy would be sure to sniff out anyone in hiding.'

'Oh, he won't be near enough for Timmy to smell out,' said Dick. 'He'll be a long way off.'

'Then how can he possibly see us – or know that we're leaving?' asked Anne.

'Anne – I don't know if you've heard of field-glasses,' began Dick, solemnly. 'Well, they're things that can spot anything half a mile away . . .'

Anne went red and gave Dick a punch. 'Don't be an ass!

Of course – that's it! Field-glasses used by someone on a hillside somewhere – trained on the old cottage.'

'Actually I think I know where the someone is,' said Dick. 'I've caught sight of a little flash every now and again on the hill yonder – the kind of flash that is made by the sun on glass – and I somehow think that our spy is sitting near the top of the hill, watching us carefully.'

Anne turned to look at the hill, but Julian at once spoke sharply. 'No – don't stand and stare up there, anyone. We don't want the watcher to know that *we* know we are being watched.'

They went on with their packing, and soon began to stagger out with their bundles. George was told to strap her things on her bicycle, and stand well out in the open as she did so, so that the watcher on the hill would be able to observe all her doings.

Julian was in the midst of carefully folding up his things to go into his knapsack, when Anne gave a sudden exclamation.

'Someone's coming!'

Everyone looked round, imagining that they would see a sinister-looking foreigner, or someone peculiar in some way.

But all they saw was a country-woman hurrying along, a shawl over her head, and a basket under her arm. She wore cheap glasses, had no make-up on, and her hair was pulled straight back under the shawl. She stopped when she saw the Five.

'Good afternoon,' said Julian, politely. 'Isn't it glorious weather!'

'Beautiful,' said the woman. 'Are you camping out – you've certainly chosen a very good time!'

'No – actually we're packing,' said Julian. 'We've been sleeping in the old cottage, but we've decided to move out. Is it very, very old?'

'Oh yes – and it's supposed to have queer things happening in it at nights,' said the woman.

'We know that!' said Julian. 'My word – we were pretty scared last night, I can tell you – weird noises and horrible, ghostly lights. We decided not to stay there any longer.'

'That's right,' said the woman. 'Don't you stay! You get as far from this place as you can! I can tell you, *I* wouldn't come by it at night. Where are you going?'

'Well, our home is at Kirrin,' said Julian, evading the question. 'You know – on Kirrin Bay.'

'Ah yes – a fine place,' said the woman. 'Well, don't you stay another night! Good-bye!'

She hurried off, and was soon lost to sight.

'Go on packing,' said Julian to the others.

'The watcher is still up in the hills. I caught sight of a flash again just then.'

'Julian – why did you tell all that to the woman?' asked Anne. 'You don't usually say so much when we are in the middle of something queer!'

'My dear, unsuspecting Anne – do you mean to say that you thought that woman was really what she pretended to be – a woman from a nearby farm?' said Julian.

'Well – wasn't she?' said Anne, surprised. 'She looked like one – no make-up – and that old shawl – and she knew all about the old cottage!'

'Anne – farm-women don't have gold fillings in their teeth,' said Julian. 'Didn't you notice them when she smiled?'

'And her hair was dyed,' said George. 'I noticed it was blonde at the roots and black above.'

'*And* what about her hands?' said Dick. 'A farmer's wife does a great deal of hard, rough work, and her hands are never white and smooth – they are rough and brown. This woman's hands were as white as a princess's!'

'Well yes – I did notice them,' said Anne. 'And I did notice too that she sometimes spoke like a country-woman and sometimes not.'

'Well, there you are!' said Julian. 'She's one of the unpleasant gang that tried to scare us last night – and when the watcher on the hill reported that we appeared to be packing up and going, she was told to go and make sure. So she pretended to be a country-woman and came by – but unfortunately we weren't quite so stupid as she thought we would be!'

'You certainly stuffed her up well!' said Dick, with a grin. 'The gang will be down here tonight, digging up all the big stones they can find. You and I will have a marvellous time, snooping round them.'

'You'll be careful they don't see you, won't you?' said Anne. 'Where will you hide?'

'We haven't planned that yet,' said Dick. 'Now – come on and we'll make a new camp somewhere that won't be easily seen. You and George and Timmy can sleep there tonight, and Ju and I will come and watch here.'

'I want to come too,' said George at once. 'Anne will be all right with Timmy.'

'You aren't joining us this time, George,' said Ju. 'The fewer people watching, the better. Sorry, old thing – but you'll have to stay with Anne.'

George scowled and looked sulky at once. Julian laughed and slapped her on the shoulder. 'What a *lovely* scowl! One of your best! I haven't seen it for quite a long time. Keep it up, George – go on, scowl a bit harder, it suits you!'

George grinned unwillingly, and pulled herself together. She hated being left out of anything – but she did see that it was no use having a crowd of people watching that night. All right – she would stay with Anne and keep her company.

It seemed as if the watcher on the hills must have gone, because there were no more sudden flashes such as came when he lifted his field-glasses to watch the Five.

'That disguised country-woman has convinced the watcher that we're going! Any ideas, anyone, where we can go? Not too far away – but somewhere where the watcher can't follow us with his glasses, if he's still up there.'

'I know a place,' said George. 'There's a simply colossal gorse-bush on the other side of the spring. And underneath it is all hollow and dry. It's almost like a kind of gorse-cave.'

'Sounds all right,' said Julian. 'Let's go and find it.'

George led the way, trying to remember exactly where it was. Timmy followed, still in his enormous cardboard collar, which was now rather the worse for wear. George stopped when they had gone a little way past the spring.

'It was somewhere here,' she said. 'I know I could still hear the sound of the spring when I found the hollow under the bush. Ah – there it is!'

It certainly was a great bush, green and spiky outside, with a few yellow blooms on it still. Under it was a big hollow place, where the ground was soft and fine, scattered with dry old prickles.

The main trunk – for it was almost a trunk that supported the big bush – was not quite in the middle, so there was a good bit of room. Julian caught hold of the branches that hid the hollow, using a folded sheet of brown paper to hold them by, for the bush was very prickly.

'This is fine,' he said. 'Plenty of room for you two girls – and Timmy. My word, he'll have difficulty with his collar though, won't he – squeezing in and out!'

'Take it off!' said Dick. 'His ear really *is* practically healed now. Even if he scratches it, he can't do much damage. Dear old Timmy, we simply shan't *know* you without your collar.'

'Right,' said George. She took a quick look at the ear. It was still covered by a piece of elastoplast, but it was quite obvious that the ear was healthy. She cut the thread that bound the two ends of the circular collar – and then bent it so that it came off.

They all stared at Timmy, who looked most surprised. He wagged his tail gently as if to say 'Well – so you've taken that thing off – I wonder why?'

'Oh Tim – you look sort of *undressed* without that collar now!' said Anne. 'It *is* nice to see you without it, though. Good old Tim! You'll guard me and George tonight, won't you? *You* know that we're in the Middle of Something again, don't you?'

'Woof,' said Timmy, wagging his tail violently. 'Woof!' Yes – he knew all right!

13

On Watch in the Cottage

It was getting dark – and under the gorse-bush it was very dark indeed! All the Five had managed to squeeze in there, and Timmy too. One torch only was allowed to be used at a time, to save the batteries of the others.

The Five were having supper. The ham was now practically finished, but there were still a few tomatoes and plenty of cake.

Julian opened the last tin of sardines, and made some sandwiches for himself and Dick to take with them. He also wrapped up two enormous chunks of cake and pocketed two slabs of chocolate each.

'We shall need something to while away the time when we're on the watch tonight!' he said, with a grin. 'I don't know if the Weepies and Wailies and Floating Lights will be along to give us a show – but I fear not. They would be wasted on an empty cottage!'

'I do hope you'll be careful,' said Anne.

'Anne – that's the seventh time you've said that,' said

Dick. 'Don't be an ass. Don't you understand that Ju and I are going to *enjoy* ourselves? You'll be the one that has to be careful.'

'How?' asked Anne, surprised.

'Well – you'll have to be careful of that big black beetle squatting over there,' said Dick. 'And mind that the hedgehog doesn't sit down on your bare legs. And be careful in case a snake wants to share this nice safe warm place with you . . .'

'Now *you're* being an ass!' said Anne, giving him a punch. 'When will you be back?'

'We shall be back at exactly the moment you hear us squeezing under here,' said Julian. 'Now Dick – what about it? I think we might be going, don't you?'

'Right,' said Dick, and began to squeeze out carefully so as not to be pricked more than he could help. 'Oh – why are gorse bushes so horribly spiteful! Jab jab – anyone would think the bush was *trying* to prick me!'

The two girls sat quite still when the boys had gone from the bush. They tried to hear their footsteps, but they couldn't. Dick and Julian trod too softly on the wiry grass.

'I do so hope they'll be . . .' began Anne, and George groaned.

'If you say that again I shall slap you, Anne! Honestly I shall.'

'I *wasn't* saying it,' said Anne, 'I was only going to say that I hope they'll be *successful* tonight. I'd like to get back to Kirrin and have some fun bathing and boating, wouldn't you?'

'Yes. And some of Joan's marvellous cooking,' said George. 'Sausages and mash – and tomatoes with it.'

'Yes. And fried plaice fresh from the sea with Joan's best chipped potatoes,' said Anne. 'I can almost smell it.'

'Woof,' said Timmy, sniffing hard.

'There! He thought I meant it!' said Anne. 'Isn't Timmy clever?'

They had a pleasant talk about how very very clever Timmy was, and Timmy listened and wagged his tail so hard that he made quite a dust in the gorse-hollow.

'Let's go to sleep,' said Anne. 'We can't talk all night – and keeping awake won't help the boys!'

They curled up on the rug they had brought and cuddled together – not so much for warmth, because it was a hot night, but because there was so little room! Anne put out her torch, and the little place immediately became black and dark. Timmy put his head on George's tummy. She groaned.

'Oh Tim – be careful, please! I had rather a lot of supper!'

Anne giggled and pulled Timmy's head close to her. It was comforting to have old Timmy there. She agreed with George that he was the best dog in the whole world.

'I wonder what the boys are doing now,' she said, after a while. 'Do you suppose they are in the middle of something exciting? Perhaps they are!'

But they weren't! Julian and Dick were feeling extremely bored at that minute. They had gone cautiously to the cottage when they had left the girls, not using their torches at all, for fear of giving anyone warning that they were about. They had debated beforehand where would be the best place to hide, and had decided that it would be a good idea to climb up the little stone stair and hide in the roofless rooms above.

'There's no roof there – and hardly any walls,' said Dick. 'We can peep over any side to watch – and no one would guess that anyone was above them, spying down! It's a good thing it's such a starry night – once we get used to the dim light, we shall be able to see fairly well. Pity there's no moon.'

They had approached the cottage very cautiously indeed, stopping at every step and listening with bated breath for any sound. But there was none.

'Not even the light of somebody's torch, either,' said Dick, in Julian's ear. 'I don't think anyone is here yet. Let's get into the cottage and up those stairs as soon as we can.'

They tiptoed into the cottage, not daring to put on their torches. They fumbled across to the little stone stairway, and climbed it with as little sound as they could. Holding their breath made their hearts thump loudly.

'Can you hear my heart thumping?' Dick whispered to Julian, as they at last stood on the floor of the roofless rooms above.

'No. Mine's just the same, thumping away! Well, we're safely here. Let's just shuffle to and fro and see if there are any loose stones we might fall over, and so give ourselves away!'

They cleared away a few loose stones, and then sat down silently on the low broken wall of the two ruined rooms. The wind blew gently but warmly. Everything was still except the rose-rambler climbing over the old house. It moved a little in the wind and made a faint scraping noise. Dick caught his hand on a thorn, and sucked his finger. The rambler was everywhere, across the floor, and over the walls and even up what was left of the little chimney!

The boys had been there for about three-quarters of an hour when Julian gave Dick a slight nudge.

'Here they come!' he whispered. 'See – over there!'

Dick looked round and about and then caught sight of a small, moving light, just a prick in the darkness. It cast a faint glow before it.

'A torch!' he whispered. 'And another – and another! Quite a procession! A slow one, too.'

The procession made very little noise. It made its way to the cottage, and then split up.

'Having a look to see if we really *are* gone,' whispered Julian. 'Hope they won't think of coming up here.'

'Let's get behind the chimney, in case,' whispered back Dick. So very quietly they rose and made their way to where the remains of the chimney stood, a dark shadow in the starry night. The chimney was quite big, though rather crumbly. The two boys crouched close to it, on the side farthest from where the stone stairway came up in the corner.

'Someone *is* coming up!' whispered Dick, his sharp ears catching the sound of someone's feet on the stone stairs. 'I hope he gets caught by the rambler – there's a big spray near the top!'

'Sh!' said Julian.

Someone came right up the stairway, and gave a sharp exclamation of annoyance near the top. 'Good!' thought Dick, 'he *has* got caught by the rambler!'

A torch shone out over the ruined rooms, the crumbling walls and the remains of the chimney. The boys held their breath, and stood like statues. The light of the torch played over the place for one second and then a voice called down the stairs.

'No one here. The kids have gone. We can get on with the job!'

The boys let out a long breath. Good – they were safe – for the time being at any rate! The visitors down below were no longer cautious – they spoke in ordinary voices and torches flashed all over the place. Then someone lighted two lanterns, and the little cottage shone quite brightly.

'Where do we start?' said a voice. 'Here, Jess – where's that plan?'

'I've got it. I'll spread it on the floor,' said a voice that

the boys recognized at once. It was the voice of the 'country-woman' who had spoken to them that day! 'Not that it's much use. Paul's no good at drawing!'

Evidently the searchers were now leaning over the plan. Voices came up the stone stairway.

'All we know for certain is that we have to find that white stone slab – and we know the size. But we don't know the place, except that we think it *must* be here. After all – we've searched the old Roman camp, and there are no slabs there that size!'

Julian nudged Dick. So some of the visitors that Guy had complained of must have been these searchers! Whatever was it they were looking for, hidden behind a slab of stone?

He knew a minute later! A drawling voice said: 'If we have to get up every great slab in this neighbourhood, we will. I'm going to find that secret way if it's the last thing I do! If we don't find that, we don't find those blueprints – and if we don't find *them*, we might as well go into the poor-house for the rest of our lives.'

'Or prison!' said someone.

'Not prison,' said the drawling voice. 'It'll be Paul who goes to prison. *He* managed to steal them, we didn't!'

'Can't you get Paul to draw a better plan than this?' said the voice of the 'country-woman'. 'I can't understand half that's written here.'

'He's ill – almost off his head, too,' said someone. 'No good asking him. He had such a time escaping with those prints, he nearly died. No good asking him, I say.'

'I can't make out this word here,' said the woman. '"W-A-D-E-R" – whatever does it mean?'

'I don't know – wait, though, I do! It might be W-A-T-E-R – water. T not D in the middle. Where's the well? Anywhere in this kitchen? That's it, that's it. *Water!* I bet there's a slab over the well. That's the way to the secret hiding-place!'

Julian clutched Dick. He was as excited as the man down below. They listened eagerly, straining their ears.

'Here's the old sink – and this must be the remains of the pump. The well's underneath this slab – and see the stone is just about the right size. Get busy! Buck up, get busy!'

14

An Exciting Night – and a Surprising Morning

Soon there came the sound of loud breathing and grunts, as the searchers tried to prise up the stone by the pump. It was obviously very heavy, and very difficult to move, for it had become almost part of the floor itself, through the centuries!

'Drat the thing! It's tearing my hands to pieces!' said a voice. 'Lend me that jemmy, Tom – you don't seem to be doing much good with it!'

After a lot more struggling and panting the stone was loosened. 'Up she comes!' said a voice, and up came the stone so suddenly that it sounded as if most of those pulling at it had sat down very hard on the floor!

The two hidden boys were beside themselves with interest and excitement. How they wished they could go and watch! But it was impossible. They must just listen and try to make out what was happening from what the men said below them.

'Is it a well down there? Yes, it is! My, the water's pretty far down – and black as pitch too.'

There was a silence as the well was examined in the light of torches. Then an exasperated voice, the one with the drawl, said: '*This* is no secret way! Who's going to get through that water! It's just an ordinary small well, and nothing else. That word *can't* have meant Water.'

'All right, boss. What *does* it mean then?' said the woman. '*I* don't know. This isn't a plan, it's a riddle! Why couldn't Paul have made it clear where this stone slab is – he just goes and does a lot of scribble round it – and all we can make out is that it's on this common, somewhere near here – and the secret way is behind the slab!'

'And all we have to do is to go and look behind dozens of heavy slabs!' said someone else. 'I'm fed up. We've lifted slabs in that wretched camp – we've lifted some here – and we still don't know if we're anywhere near the right one.'

'Shut up,' said the voice of the drawler but now the voice was sharp and angry. 'If we have to pull this cottage down, if we have to lift every slab there is, if we have to take over that camp, I'll do it! I tell you, this makes all the difference between wealth and poverty! Anyone who wants to back out can do so – but he'd better be careful!'

'Now boss, now boss, don't you fly off the handle!' said the woman. 'We're all in this! We'll do all you say. Look, let's start by lifting a few more slabs. There are not so very many that are the size that Paul figured on this plan.'

Then began a boring time for the two hidden boys, as slab after slab was lifted and put back. Nothing was found under any of them, apparently.

The men went to the out-buildings too, leaving the woman in the cottage. The boys thought she had gone as well, and Julian moved a little, feeling rather cramped after being still for so long. The woman's ears must have been sharp for she called out at once.

'Who's there? Is it you, Tom?'

The boys stiffened and stood like statues. The woman said no more. It was not long before the men came back, talking among themselves. It sounded as if there were three of them.

'No go,' said the drawler. 'I think we'll have to search that camp really well again.'

'That's going to be difficult with someone already there,' said the woman.

'We'll deal with him,' said a voice, grimly. Julian frowned. Did that mean that Guy was in danger? He had better warn him!

'I'm fed up with this place,' said the woman. 'Let's go. I don't think the slab is anywhere here! We're wasting our time!'

To the boys' great relief, the four searchers left the cottage and went off together. Julian and Dick leaned over the crumbling wall of the room they stood in, and watched the lights of the torches and lanterns getting dimmer and dimmer over the common. Good! Now they could go back to the girls!

'I'm stiff!' said Dick, stretching himself.

'Well, Ju – we know a lot more now, don't we? It's clear that someone called Paul has stolen some valuable blueprints of something – maybe a new plane, or battleship perhaps – and has hidden them in some secret place he knew of about here – and to get to it you have to lift a slab of stone of a certain size.'

'Yes. And we know the size because we've already seen the one they lifted in the old stables,' said Julian. 'I vote we go there and measure it – or measure the one by the sink. I should think that the right slab will be somewhere in the old camp. We'd better tell Guy and let him into the secret. He'll help us to search!'

'What a peculiar business this is to find ourselves mixed up in,' said Dick. 'All because George didn't like people laughing at old Timmy with a cardboard collar round his neck! Timmy's the cause of this!'

The boys went down the stone stairs, and, of course, Dick quite forgot about the rambler, which caught him neatly round the ankle and almost tripped him headlong down the stairs!

'Blow!' he said, clutching Julian and nearly making him topple too. 'Sorry. It was that rambler again. It's ripped my ankle all round. Put on the torch for goodness' sake.'

They carefully measured the stone slab by the sink and then made their way out of the cottage and up towards the spring, hoping that they would find the great gorse-bush in the dark. They tried to get under the wrong one at first, but at last found the right one. They heard a small welcome bark from Timmy.

'Oh! Julian! Dick! Is it you?' said Anne's voice, as the boys squeezed through into the hollow middle. 'Oh, what AGES you've been! We haven't slept a wink. Keep still, Timmy, do – this place is too small for you to rampage about in!'

The boys settled down and torches were put on. Julian related the curious happenings to the two interested girls. George was thrilled.

'Oh I *say*! Fancy all this springing up out of the blue so suddenly! What are you going to do?'

'Warn Guy first thing in the morning – and then get in touch with the police, I think,' said Julian. 'We ourselves can't stop the men searching the camp, and as soon as they *do* find the slab they're looking for, they can easily get what they want and go off with it!'

'Well, it's really thrilling,' said George. 'I wish I'd been with you. I'll never go to sleep tonight!'

But they did manage to drop off to sleep, for they were all very tired. After a few hours, just as dawn was breaking, Timmy lifted his head and growled. George awoke at once.

'What is it, Tim? I can't hear anything.'

But Timmy could, that was certain. George woke Julian, and made him listen to Timmy's continuous growling.

'What do you think he's growling at?' she asked. 'He keeps on and on. I can't hear a thing, can you?'

'No,' said Julian, listening. 'Well, it's no use my creeping out and going searching in the dark for whatever Timmy's growling at. It might be something silly like a weasel or a hedgehog or a stoat. Shut up, Tim. That's enough.'

Although it was as dark as night under the thick old gorse-bush, outside it was just getting light. What *was* Timmy growling at? Were there people about again? Or was it just one of the hedgehogs he so heartily disliked?

He stopped growling at last and put his head down on his paws, closing his eyes. George patted him.

'Well, whatever it was, it's gone. Are you comfy, Julian? It's very cramped in here – and hot too, isn't it?'

'Yes. We'll get up fairly early and go to warn Guy – then we'll have a swim,' said Julian, yawning. He switched off his torch and went to sleep again.

It was late when they awoke. Dick was the first, and he looked at his watch. He gave an exclamation.

'Gosh! It's half past eight! Hey, Ju – Anne – George – wake up, it's almost afternoon!'

Everyone felt stiff and cramped, and they went off to have a swim and to warn Guy. As they came near the camp, they stopped in amazement.

Someone was howling down in the trench, howling so miserably and so broken-heartedly that the Five felt quite panic-stricken. Whatever in the world could have happened? They ran to the edge of the excavations and looked down into the trench.

The boy was there, lying on his face, sobbing. He kept lifting his head and howling, then putting it down again.

'Guy! GUY! Whatever's happened?' shouted Julian. He leapt down beside the boy. 'Are you hurt? Is Jet hurt? What's the matter?'

'It's Guy! He's gone! They've taken him,' howled the

boy. 'And I was so awful to him. Now he's gone. He'll never come back, I know he won't!'

'Guy's gone? But – but *you're* Guy!' said Julian in astonishment. 'What do you mean?'

He felt sure that the boy really *was* mad now – quite mad – talking about himself like that. He patted him on the shoulder. 'Look – you're ill. You come along with us. You need a doctor.'

The boy sprang to his feet, his face swollen and stained. 'I'm not ill! I tell you Guy's gone. I'm *not* Guy. He's my twin. There are two of us.'

Everyone gasped. It took half a minute to think about this and get everything straight – and then, of course many things were clear! There was not one mad boy, there were two ordinary boys – but they were twins! There wasn't, as they had thought, just *one* boy who contradicted himself all the time, who seemed continually to appear suddenly and unexpectedly, and who was sometimes nice and sometimes not.

'Twins! Why on earth didn't we think of that before?' said Julian. 'We thought there was only one of you. You were never together.'

'No. We quarrelled – quarrelled bitterly,' said the boy, tears in his eyes again. 'And when twins quarrel, *really* quarrel, it's worse than any quarrel there is! We hated one another then – we really did! We wouldn't be with one another, we wouldn't eat together, or dig together, or sleep together. We've often quarrelled before, but not like this – not like this! I just pretended that he didn't exist – and he did the same with me!'

'What a to-do!' said Julian, astonished and worried. 'Well now – what's happened to make you so upset? Tell me!'

'Guy wanted to be friends with me again last night,' said the boy. 'And I wouldn't. I hit him and walked away.

Then this morning I was sorry and went to find him and be friends – and – and . . .'

He stopped and howled again. Everyone felt very sad and uncomfortable. 'Go on, tell us,' said Julian, gently.

'I was just in time to see him fighting two men, and screaming at them, and kicking – then they hustled him away somewhere!' said the boy. 'I fell down in the trench and hurt my leg – and by the time I dragged myself up, Guy had gone – and so had everyone else!'

He turned away and wept again. 'I'll never forgive myself, never! If I'd made friends last night I could have helped him – and I didn't!'

15

Well Done, George!

It was Anne who comforted the boy. She went to him and pulled him down on a stone beside her. 'Let me look at your leg,' she said. 'It's pretty bad, isn't it? Look, I'll bind it up for you. Don't be so upset – we'll help you. I think we know what's happened, don't we Julian?'

The boy looked at Anne gratefully, and sniffed hard. When she offered him her handkerchief, he took it and wiped his face. Dick gave Anne his big hanky to bind up the boy's cut and bruised leg. He must have fallen right into the trench in his fright at seeing his brother fighting and being taken away.

'How do *you* know what's happened?' he said to Julian. 'Can you get Guy back? Do say you can! I'll never forgive myself for this. My twin-brother – and I wasn't there to fight by his side when he needed me!'

'Now don't soak my hanky all over again!' said Anne. He gave her a forlorn little smile and turned to Julian again.

'My name's Harry Lawdler, and Guy and I are mad on old camps and buildings and things. We spend almost all our holidays together, digging and finding all kinds of things, like these.' He nodded his head towards the little shelf of relics that the four had seen before.

'Yes – Guy told us,' said Dick. 'But he never said a word about you. We were often very puzzled – we thought you and he were one boy – not two, you see – and we couldn't understand a lot of things you both said. You're so very, very alike.'

'Well – I tell you, we each pretended that the other didn't even exist,' said Harry. 'We're like that. We love each other best in the world, and we hate each other worse – when we quarrel. We're simply *horrible* then!'

'Can you tell us a bit about the people that Guy was fighting?' asked Dick.

'Yes. They were some that came before, wanting Guy to clear out while they had a look round,' said Harry, wiping his face again. 'Guy was pretty rude to them. In fact I heard him say that if they messed about his camp he would throw stones at them – he's like that, you know, very fierce, when he's roused.'

'And you think these were the same people?' said Dick. 'Which way did they go with Guy?'

'That way,' said Harry, pointing. 'I've hunted the whole camp round, but they're gone – disappeared into thin air! It's extraordinary!'

'Let's have a hunt round,' said Julian. 'We might find something. But I imagine that the searchers have taken Guy off with them because he knew too much – perhaps they found here what they were looking for, and saw Guy watching.'

'Oh! Then we're too late!' said George, in deep disappointment. 'They've got what they want – and they'll disappear now and never be caught. I expect by now they are speeding away in a fast car – and have taken Guy with them to make sure he doesn't talk before they're safely in another country!'

'Oh no!' cried Harry. 'He's not kidnapped, is he? Don't say that!'

'Come on – let's have a hunt,' said Julian, and they all made their way among the various trenches and pits, looking for they hardly knew what.

They gave it up after a while. There were too many slabs and stones of all sizes! Besides, what good would it be even if they found the right one? The birds had flown – presumably with what they had come for! In fact, if Guy hadn't come along and seen the searchers, nobody would even have known that they had been in the camp and made a successful search!

'It's no good,' said Julian, at last. 'This is too big a place to know where to look for anything that might help us. Let's go back to the gorse-bush and collect our things, return to Kirrin and go to the police. It's the only sensible thing left to do!'

'Come along, Harry,' said Anne, to the miserable twin. He was so full of remorse that her handkerchief was now soaked for the third time! 'You'd better come with us and tell all you know.'

'I'll come,' said Harry. 'I'll do anything to get Guy back. I'll never quarrel with him again. Never. To think that . . .'

'Now don't go all through that again,' said Anne. 'Look, you're upsetting Timmy so much that his tail is down all the time!'

Harry gave another forlorn little smile. They all left the camp and made their way back to the gorse-bush. It was only when they got there, and began pulling out the tins of food, as well as the rug and other things, that they realized how extremely hungry they were!

'We've had no breakfast. We've been up for ages, and it's very late. I'm simply starving!' said George.

'Well, if we finish up all the food, we shan't have to carry the tins!' said Dick. 'Let's have a meal. Ten minutes more here can't make much difference.'

They were thankful not to have to sit under the gorse-bush again. They sat outside in the sun, and discussed everything.

'I believe when Timmy began to growl and growl about six o'clock this morning, it was because he could hear those people coming quietly by to go to search the camp,' said George.

'I think you're right,' said Julian. 'I bet they searched the camp well – till Guy woke and came on the scene and fought like fury. It's a pity I didn't squeeze out from under the bush and follow them, when Timmy growled.'

'Anyone want a drink?' said George. 'I'll go and fetch some water from the spring. Where's the pineapple tin?'

Anne passed it to her. George got up and took the little rabbit path that led to the spring. She could hear it gurgling and bubbling as she came near – a very pleasant noise.

'Water always sounds nice,' said George to herself. 'I love the sound of water.'

Water! Now why did that ring a bell in her mind just then? Who had been talking about water? Oh – Dick and Julian, of course, when they had come back from the old cottage last night. They had told Anne and herself about the word on the plan – the word that might have been WATER, not WADER.

'I wonder which it was,' said George to herself as she idly held the pineapple tin to the gurgling water. She gazed at the beautiful little spring, jutting up from the stony slabs – and then another bell rang loudly in her mind.

114

'Stone slabs! Water! Why – I wonder – I just wonder – if one of *these* slabs is the one! This one just here is about the right size!'

She stared at it. It was set firmly in a high little bank at the back of the place where the spring gurgled up and then ran into the clean stony channel. *Did* it hide anything behind it?

George suddenly dropped the tin and ran back to the others at full speed. 'Julian! Julian! I believe I've found the slab! It's been staring us in the face the whole time!'

Julian was very startled. So were the others. They stared up at George in astonishment.

'What do you mean, George?' said Julian, jumping to his feet. 'Show me!'

Followed by everyone, George ran back to the spring. She pointed to the white slab behind the water. 'There!' she said. 'That's the right size, isn't it? And it's beside WATER – just as it said in the plan you told us about – only the people thought it was WADER.'

'Gosh – I wonder if you're right, George,' said Julian, excited. 'You might be – you never know. Sometimes springs come from underground passages – secret hidden ways into the earth.'

'Let's try and move it,' said Dick, his face red with sudden excitement. 'It looks pretty hefty to me.'

They began to struggle with the stone, getting extremely wet as they splashed about in the spring. But nobody minded that. This was too exciting for words. Harry helped too, heaving and tugging. He was very strong indeed.

The stone slab moved a little. It slid to one side and stuck. More tugging. More pulling. More panting and puffing!

'I believe we'll have to get help,' said Julian at last. 'It really is too heavy and well-embedded.'

'I'll go and get some of my tools,' said Harry. 'I'm used to heaving stones about with them. We can easily move it if we have the right tools.'

He flew off at top speed. The others sat down and mopped their streaming foreheads.

'Phew!' said Julian. 'What a job this is for a hot day! I'm glad Harry remembered his tools. Just what we want!'

'How queer that he and Guy are twins!' said George. 'I never even thought of such a thing!'

'Well, they behaved so idiotically,' said Julian. 'Always pretending there was just one of them, and neither of them even mentioning the other. I wonder where Guy has been taken to. I don't think he'll come to much harm – but it will be worrying to his people.'

'Here comes Harry,' said Anne, after a pause. 'One of us ought to have gone with him to help him. He's brought dozens of tools!'

The things he had fetched proved very useful indeed, especially a big jemmy-like tool. The stone soon began to move when this was applied by Julian and Harry!

'It's slipping – it's coming away – look out, it will fall right down into the spring!' cried Dick. 'Look out, you girls!'

The stone was prised right out, and fell into the stony channel where the water ran. The five children stared at the opening it left.

Julian leaned forward and looked into it. 'Yes – there's a big hole behind,' he said. 'Let me shine my torch in.'

In great excitement he flashed his torch into the opening. He turned round, his face glowing.

'Yes! I think we've got it! There's a tunnel behind, going down and down. It widens out behind this hole!'

Everyone was too thrilled for words. George gave Dick a punch, and Anne patted Timmy so hard that he whined. Harry beamed round, all his woes forgotten.

116

'Do we go down now?' asked Dick. 'We'll have to make the opening a bit wider. Earth and roots have narrowed it very much. Let's make it bigger.'

'Then we'll explore it!' said George, her eyes shining. 'A secret tunnel only known to us! Quick – let's explore it!'

16

The Secret Way

All the children were so excited that they got into each other's way. Julian pushed them back.

'Let's be sensible! We can't *all* make the opening wider – let Harry and me get at it with the tools – and we'll soon make it bigger!'

It took only a minute to hack away at the sides of the hole to make it big enough for even Julian to climb through. He stood there panting, smiling broadly.

'There – it's done! I'll get in first. Everyone got torches? We shall need them! It's going to be dark in there!'

He clambered up and into the hole. He had to crawl on hands and knees for a little way, and then the hole suddenly went downwards and became considerably bigger. Julian could walk in it, if he bent down, for at that point the tunnel was about three feet high.

He called back to the others. 'Follow me! Take hold of each other's coats or jerseys and hang on. It's as dark as pitch in here!'

George followed after Julian, then Anne, then Dick, then Harry. Timmy went with George, of course, pushing and shoving like all the rest. Everyone was excited, and nobody could talk in a normal voice. They all shouted!

'I'll give you a hand! One good shove and you're in!'

'I say – isn't it dark!'

'What a crawl! I feel like a fox going into its den!'

'Timmy, don't butt me from behind like that! I can't crawl any faster!'

'Ah – thank goodness I can stand up now! What size of rabbit do you think made *this* burrow!'

'It was made by water at some time perhaps. Don't *shove*, Timmy!'

'Water doesn't run uphill, ass! Hang on to my coat, Harry. Don't get left behind.'

Julian, bent almost double at times, walked carefully along the narrow tunnel, which went steadily downwards. Soon it widened and became higher, and then it was easier to walk in comfort.

'Do you suppose this is the right secret way?' called George, after a time. 'We don't seem to be getting anywhere.'

'I can't tell. In fact we shan't know till we find something hidden somewhere – if we ever do!'

A sudden scuttering noise in front of him made Julian stop suddenly. Immediately everyone bumped into the one in front, and there were shouts at once.

'What's up, Ju?'

Julian's torch shone on to two pairs of bright, frightened eyes. He gave a laugh.

'It's all right – just a couple of rabbits using our burrow! There are small holes running out of the tunnel which, I imagine, are rabbit burrows. I bet we're giving the bunnies a shock!'

The tunnel wound about a good deal, and then suddenly the rather soft ground they were treading on turned to rock. The passage was now not so high, and the children had to bend down again. It was most uncomfortable.

Julian stopped once more. He had heard another sound. What was it?

'Water!' he said. 'There must be an underground stream here! How thrilling! Everyone all right?'

'Yes!' shouted those behind him. 'Get on, Julian – let's see the water!'

The tunnel suddenly ended, and Julian found himself in a big cave with a fairly high roof. Almost in the middle of it ran a stream – not a very big one, and not a very fast one. It gurgled along in a small channel of rock, which it had carved out for itself through hundreds of years.

Julian shone his torch on it. The water looked very black and glittered in the light of the torch. The others came one by one out of the tunnel and stared at the underground stream. It looked rather mysterious, slipping through the cave, gurgling quietly as it disappeared through a hole at one end.

'Queer,' said Dick.

'It's not unusual, this,' began Harry. 'In some parts of the country round about here, the ground below our feet is honeycombed with many little streams. Some come up as springs, of course, some join other streams when they come out into the open, others just run away goodness knows where!'

Julian was looking up round the cave. 'Does our tunnel end here?' he wondered. 'Is this where we have to look for whatever is hidden?'

'We'll have a look round the cave and see if there are any exits,' said Dick. Using their torches the five separated, Timmy keeping close to George, not seeming in the least surprised at this underground adventure.

'I've found another tunnel over here, leading out of the

cave!' called Dick. No sooner had he said that than Anne
called out too.

'There's one here as well!'

'Now – which do we take?' said Julian. 'How annoying
that there should be two!'

'Would the fellow – what's his name – Paul – have
marked the correct underground way on his plan?' said
George. 'I mean – I don't see how he could possibly
expect either himself or anyone else to find what he had
hidden, if there are numbers of passages to choose from
down here!'

'You're right!' said Julian. 'Let's look about and see if
we can find anything to help us.'

It wasn't long before Dick gave another shout. 'It's all
right! This is the passage to take, over here – the one I
found just now. There's an arrow drawn in white chalk on
the wall.'

Everyone crowded over to Dick, stepping across the
little stream as they did so. Dick held his torch up and they
all saw the white arrow, drawn roughly on the wall.

Julian was pleased. 'Good. That helps a lot! It shows
we're going the right way – and that this *is* the secret way
that Paul chose. Come on!'

They entered the tunnel, left the little stream behind,
and went on again. 'Anyone got any idea in which direction we're going?' called Dick. 'East, west, north,
south?'

Harry had a compass. He looked at it. 'I think we're
going rather in the direction of the old Roman camp,' he
said.

'Ah – that's interesting,' said Julian. 'This tunnel was
probably used in olden times.'

'Guy and I have seen the plan of the camp as it probably
used to be,' said Harry. 'And there are plenty of tunnels
and caves and holes shown on it – just roughed in, not a

proper plan of them. Gosh – I never thought I'd be exploring one! My father warned me not to, in case of roof-falls and things like that.'

The tunnel suddenly forked into two. One passage was nice and wide, the other narrow. Julian took the wide one, thinking that the other was really too narrow to get through. But after a minute or two, he stopped, puzzled.

'There's a blank wall of rock here – the tunnel's ended! We'll have to turn back! I suppose we should have taken that very narrow opening.'

They went back, Harry leading the way now. Timmy suddenly took it into his head that *he* would like to lead, too, and made himself a real nuisance, pushing his way between everyone's legs!

They came back to the fork. Harry shone his torch in at the second opening, the very narrow one. There, clearly marked on the right hand wall, was a white arrow in chalk!

'We're idiots,' said Dick. 'We don't even look for the sign-posts! Lead the way, Julian!'

This tunnel was very narrow indeed, and had rough, jutting rocky sides. There were loud 'Aahs!' and 'Oohs!' as elbows and ankles were knocked against hard rock.

And then again there came a blank wall of rock in front of Julian, and again he had to stop!

'Can't go this way either!' he said. 'There's a blank wall again – this is a blind alley too!'

There were cries of dismay at once.

'Blow! It can't be!'

'What's gone wrong? Look all round, Ju – flash your torch down at your feet and above your head!'

Julian shone his torch over his head, and gave an exclamation.

122

'There's a hole above my head!'

'Is there a white arrow anywhere?' called Harry.

'Yes! And it's pointing up, instead of forwards!' called back Julian. 'We're still all right – we've got to go up-wards now – but how?'

George, who was just behind him, shone her torch on the side-walls. 'Look!' she said. 'We can easily get up to the hole. There are rough, natural steps up – made by ledges of rock. Look, Julian!'

'Yes,' said Julian. 'We can manage to get up quite easily, I think. George, you go first – I'll give you a boost up.'

George was delighted to go first. She put her torch between her teeth, and began to climb up the ledges, Julian pushing her as best he could. She came to the hole and immediately saw that it would be quite easy to hoist herself through.

'One more boost and I'll be through!' she called to Julian. And with one last heave George was up, rolling on the floor of a small cave above! She called down in excitement to the others.

'I believe this is the place where those things are hidden! I can see something on a ledge. Oh, do buck up!'

The others followed eagerly. Dick slipped off the rocky ledges in his excitement and almost squashed poor Harry as he fell on him. However, everyone was up at last, even Timmy, who was the most difficult of all to heave through! He seemed to have far too many vigorous legs!

Harry found no difficulty at all. 'I'm used to this kind of thing,' he said. 'Guy and I have explored a whole lot of tunnels and caves in hills and other places.'

George was pointing her torch at a broad ledge of rock. On it was a brown leather bag, and beside it, marked on the rock, was a very large arrow indeed.

Julian was overjoyed. He picked up the bag at once.

'My word – I hope there's something in it!' he said. 'It feels jolly light – as if it's empty!'

'Open it!' cried everyone – but Julian couldn't. It was locked – and alas, there wasn't a key!

17

Full of Surprises

'It's locked – we can't open the bag,' said Julian, and shook it vigorously as if that might make it fly open and spill whatever contents it had!

'We don't know if it's got anything of value in it or not,' said Dick, in deep disappointment. 'I mean – it might be some trick on that fellow Paul's part – he might have taken the blue-prints, or whatever they were he hid, for himself, and left the bag just to trick the others.'

'Can we cut it open?' asked George.

'No. I don't think so. It's made of really strong leather. We would need a special knife to cut through it – an ordinary pen-knife wouldn't be any use,' said Julian. 'I think we'll just have to assume that we've got the goods, and hope for the best. If they're not in here, it's just bad luck. Someone else has got them, if so.'

They all looked at the tantalising bag.

Now they would have to wait for ages before they found out whether their efforts had been successful or not!

'Well – what do we do now?' said George, feeling suddenly flat. 'Go back all through that long tunnel once more? I'll be glad to be in the open air again, won't you?'

'Rather!' said Julian. 'Well – I suppose we'd better get down through that hole again.'

'Wait!' said Anne, her sharp eyes catching sight of something. 'Look – what does all this mean?'

She shone her torch on to various signs on the wall. Again there were arrows drawn in white chalk – but very oddly, a line of them ran downwards across the wall of the little rocky room, right to the edge of the hole – and another line of arrows pointing the *other* way, ran horizontally across the wall!

'Well – do you suppose that's just meant to muddle people?' said Dick, puzzled. 'We know jolly well that the way out of this room is down that hole, because that's the way we came into it.'

'Perhaps the other line of arrows means that there's a second way out,' suggested George. They all looked round the little rocky room. There didn't seem any way out at all.

'Where's Timmy?' said Anne, suddenly, flashing her torch round. 'He's not here! Has he fallen down the hole? I never heard him yelp!'

At once there was a great to-do. 'Timmy, Timmy, Timmy! TIMMY! Where are you?'

George whistled shrilly, and the noise echoed round and round the little room. Then, from somewhere, there was a bark. How relieved everyone was.

'Where is he? Where did that bark come from?' said Dick. 'It didn't sound as if it came from below, down that hole!'

There came another welcome bark, and the sound of Timmy's feet. Then to everyone's amazement, he appeared in the little rocky room as if by magic – appearing straight out of the wall, it seemed!

'Timmy! Where were you? Where have you come from?' cried George, and ran to see. She came to a standstill and exclaimed loudly.

'Oh! What idiots we are! Why, just behind this big jutting-out piece of rock, there's another passage!'

So there was! A very, very narrow one, it is true – and completely hidden from the children because of the enormous slab of rock that jutted out from the wall that hid it! They stood and stared at it, shining their torches on the narrow way. The arrows ran round the wall to it.

'We never even looked properly!' said Dick. 'Still – it's a passage that would be extremely difficult to spot – hidden round the corner of that rock – and very narrow at that. Well, I do know one thing for certain about that man called Paul!'

'What?' asked Anne.

'He's thin – thin as a rake!' said Dick. 'No one but a skinny fellow could squeeze through *this* opening! I doubt if *you* can, Julian – you're the biggest of us.'

'Well, what about trying?' said George. 'What does everyone say? This might be an easier, shorter way out – or it might be a harder, longer one.'

'It won't be longer,' said Harry. 'By my reckoning we must be pretty well near the Camp now. It's likely that the way leads straight there – though where it comes out I can't imagine. Guy and I have explored the Camp pretty thoroughly.'

Dick suddenly thought of something he had noticed at the Camp – the big hole behind the slab of stone, where he had seen the baby rabbit a day or two before! What had Guy said about that? He had said there was a great hole underground, which had been explored – but that it was probably just an ancient storage place for food or for loot! He turned eagerly to Harry.

'Harry – would this lead to that enormous hole underground – the one that Guy once told me had been explored, but was of no interest – probably just an old store-place?'

'Let me see,' said Harry. 'Yes – yes, it *might* lead to that. Most of these underground ways are through-ways – ways that lead from one place to another. They don't as a rule stop suddenly, but have usually been of use as secret escape-routes or something of that kind. I think you may be right, Dick – we're fairly near the Camp, I'm sure, and we may quite well find that if we go on, instead of going back, we shall come into the Camp itself – probably through that great hole!'

'Then come on,' said Julian. 'It will certainly be a shorter way!'

They tried to squeeze through the narrow opening that led out of the little rocky room. Dick got through all right, and so did the others – but poor Julian found it very very difficult and almost gave up.

'You shouldn't eat so much,' said Dick, unkindly. 'Go on – one more try, Ju – I'll haul on your arm at the same time!'

Julian got through, groaning. 'I'm squashed flat!' he said. 'Now, if anyone makes any more jokes about too much breakfast, I'll pull his nose!'

The passage grew wider immediately, and everyone was thankful. It ran fairly straight, and then went steeply downwards, so that the five slithered about, and Timmy found himself suddenly running. Then it came to a stop – a complete stop! This time it was not a blank wall of rock that faced them – it was something else.

'A roof-fall!' groaned Dick. 'Look at that! Now we're done!'

It certainly looked most formidable. Earth, rocks and stones had fallen from the roof and blocked up the whole passage-way. There was no use in going on – they would just have to turn and go back!

'Blow it!' said Dick, and kicked at the mass of earth. 'Well – there's no use staying here – we'd better turn back. My torch isn't too good now, and neither is yours, George. We don't want to lose any time – if our torches give out, we shall find things very difficult.'

They turned to go back, feeling very despondent. 'Come on, Timmy!' said George. But Timmy didn't come. He stood beside the roof fall, looking very puzzled, his ears cocked and his head on one side. Then he suddenly gave a sharp bark.

It made everyone jump almost out of their skins, for the sound echoed round and about in a very queer way.

'Don't, Timmy!' said George, almost angrily. 'Whatever's the matter? Come along!'

But Timmy didn't come. He began to paw at the pile of earth and rocks in front of him, and barked without stopping. Wuff-wuff-wuff-wuff-wuff-WUFF!

'What's up?' said Julian, startled. 'Timmy, what on *earth's* the matter?'

Timmy took absolutely no notice, but went on feverishly scraping at the roof-fall, sending earth and stones flying all over the others.

'There's something he wants to get at – something behind this roof-fall,' said Dick. 'Or perhaps *somebody* – make him stop barking, George, and we'll listen ourselves and see if we can hear anything.'

George silenced Timmy with difficulty, and made him stand quiet and still. Then they all listened intently – and a sound came at once to their ears.

'Yap-yap-wuff-wuff-wuff!'

'It's Jet!' yelled Harry, making everyone jump violently again. 'Jet! Then Guy must be with him. He never leaves

Guy! What's Guy doing here? He may be hurt. GUY! GUY! JET!'

Timmy began to bark wildly again and to scrape more furiously than ever. Julian shouted to the others above the barking.

'If we can hear Jet barking, this roof-fall can't be very big. We'd better try and get through it. Two of us can work in turn with Timmy. We can't all work at once, the passage is too narrow.'

Then began some very hard work – but it didn't last as long as Julian feared, because, quite suddenly, the mass of rubble and rock shifted as they worked, and a gap appeared at the top of the heap, between it and the roof.

Dick began to scramble up, but Julian called to him at once. 'Be careful, ass! The roof can't be too good here – it may come down again, and you'll be buried. Go carefully!'

But before Dick could go any further, a little figure appeared on the top of the rubble over their heads, and slid down to them yapping loudly, and waving a long wiry tail!

'Jet! Oh, Jet! Where's Guy?' cried Harry, as the little dog leapt into his arms and licked his face lavishly, barking joyfully in between the licks.

'GUY!' yelled Julian. 'Are you there?'

A weak voice came back. 'Yes! Who's that?' An absolute volley of voices answered him.

'It's us! And Harry! We're coming to you, we shan't be long!'

And it wasn't long, either, before the roof-fall was slowly and carefully climbed by each one – though Timmy, of course, scrambled up, over and down at top speed!

On the other side of the roof-fall was a passage, of course, the continuation of the one the children had come along. Guy was there, sitting down, looking very pale. Jet flung himself on him and licked him as if he hadn't seen him for a month, instead of just a minute or two before!

'Hallo!' said Guy, in a small voice. 'I'm all right. It's just my ankle, that's all. I'm jolly glad to . . .'

But before he could say a word more, Harry was beside him, his arms round him, his voice choking.

'Guy! Oh, Guy! I've been a beast. I wouldn't be friends!

What happened to you? Are you really all right? Oh Guy, we *are* friends again, aren't we?'

'Look out Harry, old son,' said Julian gently. 'He's fainted. Now just let's be sensible and everything will come all right. Flap your hanky at him, Dick, and give him a little air. It's only the excitement!'

In half a minute Guy opened his eyes and smiled weakly. 'Sorry!' he said. 'I'm all right now. I only hope this isn't a dream, and that you really *are* here!'

'You bet we are!' said Dick. 'Have a bit of chocolate, then you'll know we're real!'

'Good idea!' said Julian. 'We'll all have some – and I've some biscuits in my pocket too. We'll eat and talk – and we'll make plans at the same time. Catch, Guy – here's a biscuit!'

18

The Way Out

Guy soon told his story. It was much as the others had imagined.

'I was fast asleep this morning, with Jet curled up to me,' he said. 'He began to bark and I wondered why, so I got up to see – and I saw four people in the camp.'

'The four we know!' said Dick, and Julian nodded. 'Go on, Guy.'

'They were looking all over the place,' said Guy, 'prising up rocks, messing about – so I yelled at them. But they only laughed. Then one of the men, who was trying to prise up a slab – the slab that covers that great hole underground, Harry – you remember it? – well, this man gave a yell and said "I've got it! This is the way in – down here, behind this slab!"'

Guy stopped, looking very angry. Jet licked him comforting. 'Well,' he went on, 'I set Jet on them, and they kicked him cruelly – so I went for them.'

'You're a plucky one, aren't you!' said Dick, admiringly. 'Did you knock them all out, by any chance?'

'No. Of course not,' said Guy. 'One of the men pretty well knocked *me* out though. He hit me on the head and I went down, dazed. I heard him say "drat this kid – he'll be fetching help, and we shan't be able to get down and hunt for the goods." And then another man said "We'll take him with us then," and they got hold of me and dragged me through the opening.'

'But how did they get down into that great hole?' said Harry in wonder. 'There is such a steep drop into it. You need a rope.'

'Oh, they had a rope all right,' said Guy, munching his biscuit and chocolate and looking decidedly better. 'One of the men had one tied round and round his waist. They knotted it fast round a rock – that big one we can't move, Harry – and then they swung down on it. All except the woman. She said she'd stay at the top and keep watch. She hid behind a bush some way off.'

'I never saw her when I came along!' said Harry. 'I never thought of looking there! What about you? Did you get down too?'

'Yes. I screamed and shouted and kicked and howled, but it wasn't a bit of good. They made me swing down the rope – and I fell off half-way down and hurt my ankle. I howled at the top of my voice for help, and they hurried me along with them, shaking me like a rat.'

'The beasts!' said Harry, fervently. 'Oh, the beasts!'

'I heard one of them say that there should be a tunnel out of the hole somewhere, it was marked on Paul's plan – whatever that may be – and then I think I must have fainted – the pain of my ankle, you know. And when I came to myself again, we were all here, the three men and I – beside this roof-fall – though I really don't know how we got here. They must have dragged me along with them!'

'And that's all, is it?' asked Julian.

'Not quite. They were furious when they saw the roof-fall, but as soon as they began to scrabble in it a rock rolled down and hit one of the men quite a crack – and after that they were afraid to do anything. They stood and talked for a bit – and then they decided to go and get some tools, and come down again to see if they could remove all this stuff and get through it.'

'Good gracious!' said Julian, startled. 'Then they may be back at any moment?'

'I suppose so. They left me here because they couldn't think of anything else to do with me! They knew I couldn't walk, because of my ankle. I think it's broken. So of course, I couldn't possibly find my way out myself! And here I've been waiting for those brutes to come back, and to hack through the rubble to go after whatever it is they want!'

Everyone began to feel rather uncomfortable at the thought that three violent men might be appearing at any moment. 'Is it very far to the opening you came down?' asked Julian. But Guy didn't know. He had fainted, as he had said, and he didn't even know what way they had come.

'It can't be far,' said Harry. 'I think it would be worth while trying to find the opening, see if the men have left the ropes there, and get out that way. If Guy's ankle really is broken, he couldn't possibly manage to go back the long way we've come.'

'No. That's true,' said Julian, thoughtfully. 'Well, that's what we'll do then. But we'll go jolly cautiously, without a sound, because it might be just our luck to meet those fellows on their way back here!'

'Shall we start?' said George. 'What about Guy?'

Julian knelt down beside the boy, and gently examined his ankle. 'I've done my First Aid Training, like everybody else!' he said. 'And I *ought* to know if his ankle is broken or just sprained.'

He examined the swollen ankle carefully. 'It's not broken. I believe I could bandage it tightly with a couple of large hankies. Give me yours, Dick.'

The others watched admiringly as Julian deftly and confidently bandaged Guy's swollen ankle. 'There!' he said. 'You can perhaps hobble on it now, Guy. It may hurt, but I don't think it will damage it. Try. You'll have to go barefoot because your ankle is too swollen for your shoe to go on.'

Very gingerly Guy stood up, helped by Harry. He tried his hurt foot, and it certainly seemed all right to hobble on, though it was very painful. He grinned round at the others' anxious faces.

'It's fine!' he said. 'Come on, let's go! We don't want to bump into those fellows if we can help it. Thank goodness we've got Jet and Timmy.'

They set off down the passage, flashing their torches in front as usual, to show them the way. The tunnel was quite wide and high here, and in a very short time came out into an enormous pit underground.

'Ah – this is the hole I saw down behind the slab where the rabbit went,' said Dick. 'We weren't very far from the camp, as we thought. I'm surprised that when this pit was explored, the underground passages were not discovered, Guy!'

'I expect the men exploring it came to the roof-fall and thought there was nothing beyond,' said Guy. 'Or maybe they were afraid of going further in case of further falls. They can be very dangerous, you know. Many a man has been buried under one and never heard of again.'

They looked round the enormous hole – it was really a huge round pit. Daylight showed in the roof at one place.

'That's the opening into it,' said Guy, eagerly. 'The one I came through, on the rope.'

He limped a few steps forward to look for the rope. Harry held him by the arm, thankful that the ankle was holding up so well. Guy pointed upwards.

'Yes. I can see the rope. The men have left it there, thank goodness. They must have been certain that I couldn't get to it!'

The rope hung down from the little opening high above their heads. Julian looked round at Anne.

'Can you manage to climb up the rope, Anne?' he said, doubtfully.

'Of course!' said Anne, scornfully. 'We do rope-climbing in the gym at school often enough. Don't we, George?'

'Yes – but our gym rope is a bit thicker!' said George.

'I'll go up first,' said Harry. 'We've got a much thicker rope, Guy and I, that we use when we want to haul on very heavy stones. I'll find it, and let it down.'

'Well – we can't afford to waste any time, in case those fellows come back,' said Julian. 'I daresay the girls can manage all right. George, you go up first.'

George went up like a monkey, hand over hand, her leg twisted round the rope. She grinned down when she got to the top.

'Easy!' she said. 'Come on up next, Anne, and show the boys how to do it!'

Before the boys could leap to the rope, Anne was on it, pulling herself up lithely. Julian laughed. He called up to George.

'George! You might have a squint round and see if there's any sign of people about. If they were going to borrow *Guy's* tools, they would have been back long ago, so I think probably they've had to go to Kirrin or some farm-house to borrow them.'

'They wouldn't get my tools!' said Guy, 'or Harry's. We had them stolen once, and now we always hide them where no one can possibly find them.'

'That settles it then,' said Julian. 'They've had to go a good way, I expect, to get satisfactory tools to tackle that roof-fall. They probably imagine that it's a pretty *big* fall! All the same, keep a watch out, George, till we're all up.'

It was difficult to get Guy up, for he was feeling weak, but they managed it at last. The two dogs had to have the boys' shirts tied round them so that the rope would not cut them when they were hauled up. They didn't seem to mind at all. Timmy was very heavy to pull up because he appeared to think that he had to try and make his legs do a running action all the time – just to help! All that happened was that he began to spin round and round, as he went up!

Everyone was up in the open air at long last, hot and perspiring. Julian had the precious bag safely under his arm. Timmy sat down panting. Then he suddenly stopped panting, and pricked up his ears.

'Woof,' he said warningly, and stood up.

'Quiet, Tim, quiet, Jet,' said Julian, at once aware that somebody must be about. 'Hide, everyone – quickly. It may be those fellows coming back!'

'Wuff,' began Jet, but Guy stopped him immediately. The six children separated and went into hiding at once, each choosing the best place he or she could see. There were plenty of hiding-places in the old camp!

They heard voices coming near. Nobody dared to peep out and see who was coming – but Julian and Dick recognised the drawling voice of one of the men!

'What a time we've been!' said the man. 'Just chuck the spades and things down the hole – then we'll all climb down again. Buck up! We've wasted too much time already. Anyone might come on the scene at any moment!'

The spades and jemmies went hurtling down the hole. Then one by one the men went down the rope. The children could not hear the woman's voice. They thought she must have been left behind.

Julian gave a low whistle and all the others popped up their heads. 'We'll spring for it!' said Julian. 'Buck up!'

They all shot out of their hiding-places at once and made off – except Julian. He stayed behind for a minute or two. What *could* he be doing?

Julian was doing something very simple indeed! He was hauling up the rope that dangled underground! He slipped it off the rock that held it and tied it round his waist, looking suddenly very bulky.

He grinned a very wide grin and went after the others. How very, very angry those men were going to be!

19

Back to Kirrin Cottage

Julian ran after the others. 'What were you doing?' said George. 'Calling rude names down to the men?'

'No. I hope they'll go and dig for hours if they want to!' said Julian. 'They'll soon find that when they've got through it, that roof-fall is nothing much, and they'll go on till they come to the little room – and what they'll say when they find that the bag is gone, I really don't know!'

'I wish I could be there!' said Dick.

'What are we going to do about Guy?' asked Harry. 'He really can't walk *very* far on that bad foot.'

'If he can walk as far as the gorse-bush where we've left our things, I've got a bike there,' said George. 'He could pedal with one foot, I should think.'

'Oh yes – I could easily do that,' said Guy, pleased. He had dreaded the thought of having to walk all the way to Kirrin – but neither did he want to be left behind!

He limped along, helped by Harry, who couldn't do enough for him. Jet ran along beside them, excited and happy at being with so many people. Timmy sometimes wuffed a little bark to him, which made Jet as proud as punch. He thought the big Timmy was wonderful!

They came to the gorse-bush, and found their things all safe. The bicycle was there, with its packages strapped to it. George unstrapped them, meaning to carry them herself, so that Guy would not have too heavy a weight to pedal with his one foot. They all started off together, Guy riding ahead on the bicycle.

'We will go to Kirrin, dump our things at the cottage, and get Aunt Fanny to ring the police and ask them if they'll come along and collect this bag from us,' said Julian. 'I don't want to leave it at the police station – I want to see it opened in front of us!'

'I do hope it won't be empty,' said Anne. 'It does feel terribly light!'

'Yes. It does,' said Julian, swinging it to and fro. 'I can't help fearing that Paul, who drew the plan that the men found so difficult to understand, may have double-crossed his friends – drawn a deliberately difficult plan – and then left the bag quite empty in the place he marked on the plan! It would be the kind of hoax that a trickster loves to play – and would give him time to get away in safety.'

'But they said he was ill,' said Dick. 'Still – perhaps he might have been pretending that too! It's a mystery!'

'How are you getting on, Guy?' called George, as they overtook the boy. He kept riding on by himself for a little way, and then resting, waiting for them to catch up with him before he pedalled on again with his one good foot.

'Very well indeed, thank you,' said Guy. 'This bike was a very good idea of yours. What a blessing you had it with you!'

'Your foot doesn't seem any more swollen,' said Anne. 'I expect you'll be able to walk on it properly in a day or two. Oh, dear – it does make me laugh when I think how puzzled we all were when we thought there was just one of you, not twins!'

'We met first one of you, then the other, and thought you were the same boy,' said George, with a chuckle. 'We were absolutely wild with you sometimes, you seemed so mad and contradictory!'

'Don't remind us of it,' said Harry. 'I can't bear thinking that if I'd only been with Guy, all this trouble of his would never have happened.'

'Oh well – it's an ill wind that blows nobody any good!' said George. 'The bad and the good have fitted together very well this time, and made a most exciting adventure!'

'Here's Carters Lane at last,' said Anne. 'What a long walk it seemed over the common. It will be much easier for you to ride that bike when you're on a proper road, Guy. It won't go bumping over heather clumps now.'

They went down the long lane and came into Kirrin at last, realising that they were all very hungry indeed. 'It must be well past dinner-time,' said George, looking at her watch. 'Good gracious – it's a quarter to two! Would you believe it! I hope there's some dinner left over for us – Mother doesn't know we're coming.'

'We'll raid Joan's larder!' said Dick. 'She never minds so long as she's there to grumble at us while we do it!'

They went in at the gate of Kirrin Cottage and up to the front door, which was open. George shouted.

'Mother! Where are you? We've come back!'

Nobody answered. George yelled again. 'Mother! We've come home!'

The door of the study opened and her father looked out, red in the face and frowning.

'George! How many times am I to tell you not to shout when I'm working? Oh, my goodness me, who are all these?'

'Hallo, Father!' said George, mildly. 'Surely you know

143

Anne and Julian and Dick! *Don't* say you've forgotten them already!'

'Of course not! But who are these?' and George's father pointed to the startled twins. 'They're as like as peas. Where did *they* come from? I haven't seen them before, have I?'

'No, Father. They're just friends of ours,' said George. 'Where's Mother? We've just had an adventure and we want to tell her. Oh, and we want to ring the police – and I think we ought to get a doctor to see to Guy's foot – and Father, look, Timmy's ear is healed!'

'Bless us all! There's never any peace when you are about, George,' said her father, groaning. 'Your mother's at the bottom of the garden, picking raspberries – or it might have been strawberries.'

'Oh no, Father – it's August, not June!' said George. 'You always . . .'

Julian thought he had better get his uncle safely back in his study before a row blew up between him and George. Uncle Quentin did *not* like being disturbed in his complicated work!

'Let's go and find Aunt Fanny,' he said, 'we can tell her everything out in the garden. Come on!'

'Wuff-wuff!' said Jet.

'Good gracious – that's not *another* dog, is it?' said George's father, scowling. 'How many times have I said that . . .'

'We won't disturb you any more, Uncle,' said Julian, hurriedly, seeing Guy's scared face. 'We'll go and find Aunt Fanny.'

They all went thankfully out in the garden, hearing the house echo to the slam of Uncle Quentin's study door. George shouted.

'Mother! Where are you?'

'Shut up, George – we don't want to make your father leap out of the window after us!' said Dick. 'Ah – there's Aunt Fanny!'

His aunt was very surprised to see him and the others advancing on her. She went to greet them, a basket of raspberries on her arm.

'Well! I thought you wanted to stay away for longer than this!'

'We did – but an adventure descended on us!' said Dick. 'We'll tell you all about it in detail later on, Aunt Fanny.'

'But just now we want two things – can we ring the

police – or will *you* – and ask them to come here?' said Julian, very grown-up all of a sudden. 'There's something that might be very important for them to know. And also do you think we should let a doctor see Guy's foot – he's sprained his ankle, I think?'

'Oh dear!' said Aunt Fanny, distressed to see the boy's swollen foot. 'Yes – he ought to have that seen to properly. Who is he? Dear me – there's another of them! Aren't they alike?'

'Twins,' said George. 'I don't know how I shall be able to tell one from t'other when Guy's bad foot is better.'

'I'm going to ring the police,' said Julian, seeing that his aunt could now only think of Guy's swollen foot. He went off indoors, and they heard him speaking on the telephone. He put it down and came out again.

'The Inspector himself is coming,' said Julian. 'Shall I ring the doctor now, Aunt Fanny?'

'Oh yes. His number is 042,' said his aunt. 'How *did* you get such an ankle, Guy?'

'Mother, you don't seem at all interested in our adventure,' complained George.

'Oh, I am, dear,' said her mother. 'But you do have such a lot, you know. What have you been up to this time?'

But before George could do more than begin, a black police car drew up at the front gate, and the inspector of police got out and marched up to the front door. He knocked extremely loudly on the knocker.

Which, of course, had the immediate result of bringing George's father hotfoot out of his study in another rage! He flung open the front door.

'Hammering at the door like that! What's the matter? I've a good mind to report you to the police! Oh – er – h'm – good afternoon, Inspector. Do come in. Are we expecting you?'

Smiling broadly, the Inspector came in. By this time

Julian had come back in the house again, and greeted him. His uncle went back into his study, rather red in the face, and actually closed the door quietly!

'You wanted me to come along at once, because of something important?' said the Inspector. 'What is it?'

The others came into the room now, with Julian's aunt behind them. Julian nodded round at them. 'They're all in this, sir – except my aunt, of course. We've brought something we think may be important, sir. Quite a lot of people were looking for it – but we managed to get hold of it first!'

He put the brown bag on the table. The Inspector's eyes went to it at once. 'What is it? What's inside? Stolen goods?'

'Yes, sir – blue-prints of some kind, I think. But I don't know what of, of course.'

'Open the bag, my boy! I'll examine them,' said the Inspector.

'I can't open it,' said Julian. 'It's locked – and there's no key!'

'Well – we'll soon manage *that*!' said the Inspector, and took out a small, strong-looking tool. He forced the lock, and the bag opened. Everyone leaned forward eagerly, even Timmy. What was in the bag?

There was nothing there! Absolutely nothing! Julian groaned in bitter disappointment.

'No wonder it felt so light. It's empty after all. Would you believe it!'

20

The Adventure Ends – as it Began!

It was a moment of great disappointment for all the children. Although they had talked about the possibility of the bag being empty, everyone had secretly felt certain that something exciting would be inside.

The Inspector was astonished. He looked round sharply. 'Where did you get this bag? What made you think it had stolen goods inside – and what kind of blue-prints were they?'

'Well, sir – it's rather a long story,' said Julian.

'I'm afraid you'll have to tell it to me,' said the Inspector, taking out his notebook. 'Now – how did this all begin?'

'Well – it really began with Timmy hurting his ear and having to wear a cardboard collar,' said George.

The Inspector looked most surprised. He turned to

Julian. '*You'd* better tell it,' he said. 'I don't want to waste time on cardboard collars!'

George went red and put on a scowl. Julian grinned at her, and began the story, making it as clear and short as he could.

The Inspector became more and more interested. He laughed when Julian came to the weird noises and lights.

'They certainly wanted to get rid of you,' he said. 'You were plucky to stay on. Go on – there's something behind all this, that's certain!'

He jotted down the name of 'Paul', and 'Jess', the name of the woman. He noted that one man had a drawl. 'Any other clues to them?' he asked.

'Only this, sir,' said Julian and handed his drawing of the crêpe-soled shoe to the Inspector. This was carefully folded and put into the notebook too. 'Might be of use. Might not,' said the Inspector. 'You never know!'

He listened intently to the tale of the underground passages, and picked up the bag again.

'I can't understand why it's empty,' he said. 'It isn't really like a crook deliberately to mislead his friends when they know quite well where he is and can get at him whenever they like.' He shook the bag hard. Then he began to examine it very very carefully.

Finally he took out a sharp knife and gently slit the lining at the bottom of the bag. He turned it back.

Something was there – under the lining! Something blue, folded very carefully. Something covered with thousands of minute figures, thousands of lines, thousands of queer little designs!

'Wheeeeeew!' whistled the Inspector. 'So the bag's *not* empty, after all! Now what is this? It's a blue-print of some project – but what?'

'My father would know!' said George, at once. 'He's a scientist, you know, Inspector – one of the cleverest in the world. Shall I get him?'

'Yes,' said the Inspector, laying out the blue-print on the table. 'Get him at once.'

George flew off and returned with her father, who didn't look very pleased.

'Good afternoon, sir, once more. Sorry to disturb you,' said the Inspector. 'But do you happen to know whether this document is of any importance?'

George's father took it up. He ran his eyes over it, and then gave a loud exclamation.

'Why – why – no, it's IMPOSSIBLE! Good heavens, it's – no, no, it can't be! Am I dreaming?'

Everyone gazed at him, surprised and anxious. What did he mean? What could it be, this blue-print?

'Er – it's important then, sir?' said the Inspector.

'Important? IMPORTANT? My dear fellow, there are only two of these prints in existence – and at the moment I have the second one, which I am checking very carefully indeed. Where did this come from? Why – I simply can't believe it! Sir James Lawton-Harrison has the other. There isn't a third!'

'But – but – there must be if you have one here and Sir James has the other!' said the Inspector. 'It's obvious there is a third!'

'You're wrong. It isn't obvious!' shouted George's father. 'What *is* obvious is that Sir James hasn't got his! I'll ring him up – this very minute. Astounding! Most disturbing! Bless us all, what will happen next?'

The children did not dare say a word. They were full of astonishment. To think that the blue-print was so important – and that George's father actually had a pair to this one. What was its importance?

They heard George's father shouting into the telephone, evidently angry and disturbed. He slammed it down and came back.

'Yes. Sir James's copy has been stolen – but it's been kept very hush-hush because of its importance. Good heavens – they never even let *me* know! And to think I spilt a bottle of ink over mine yesterday – gross carelessness. Stolen! A thing like that – stolen out of his safe under his very nose. Now there's only one copy left!'

'Two, sir,' said the Inspector, tapping the copy on the table. 'You're so upset to hear that Sir James's copy has gone that you've forgotten we have it here!'

'Bless us all! Thank goodness! Yes, I *had* forgotten for

the moment!' said Uncle Quentin. 'My word, I even forgot to tell Sir James it was here.' He leapt up to go to the telephone again, but the Inspector caught his arm.

'No, sir. Don't telephone again. I think we should keep this as quiet as possible.'

'Father – what *is* this a blue-print of?' said George, voicing the thoughts of everyone there, the Inspector included.

'This blue-print? I'm certainly not going to tell you!' said her father. 'It's too big a thing even to speak of to you children – or the Inspector either for that matter. It's one of the biggest secrets we have. Here, give it to me.'

The Inspector placed his big hand on it at once. 'No, sir. I think I must take it with me, and send a secret messenger to Sir James with it. It wouldn't do to have the only two copies in one place. Why, your house might catch fire and both prints might go up in flames!'

'Take it, then, take it! We can't possibly risk such a thing!' said George's father. He glared round at the children. 'I still don't understand how *you* came to possess it!' he said, looking suddenly amazed.

'Sit down, sir, won't you, and listen to their tale,' said the Inspector. 'They've done very well. They haven't finished their story.'

Julian went on with it. The Inspector sat up straight when he heard where the three men were – down in the great pit below the Roman camp.

'You saw them go down into that pit?' he said. 'Watched them swing down on the rope? They may be there now!' He glanced at his watch. 'No, they won't. They'll be gone.'

He groaned loudly. 'And to think we might easily have caught three clever rogues. They've slipped through our hands again!'

'They haven't!' said Julian, his voice rising exultantly. 'They're still there!'

'How do you know?' said the Inspector.

'Because I pulled up their rope and took it away – look, I've got it round me!' said Julian. 'They can't get out without a rope – and they won't know how to escape any other way. They're still there – waiting for you, Inspector!'

The Inspector slapped the table so hard that everyone jumped and the two dogs barked.

'Good work!' he boomed. 'Magnificent! I must go at once and send some men out there. I'll let you know what happens!'

And out he went at a run, the precious blue-print buttoned safely in his pocket. He leapt into the driving-seat and the police-car roared away at top speed down the lane.

'Whew!' said Julian, flopping back into his chair. 'It's too exciting for words!'

Everyone felt the same, and began to talk at the tops of their voices. Poor Aunt Fanny couldn't make herself heard. But when Joan came in and asked if anyone wanted anything to eat, they heard her at once!

The doctor came to see Guy's foot, and re-bandaged it. 'Rest it for a day or two,' he said. 'It will soon be all right.'

'Well, you'll have to stay here with George and the others, Guy,' said George's mother. 'You can't go ex-cavating in that camp of yours again yet. Harry can stay too. So can Jet.'

The twins beamed. They liked this jolly family, and the adventurous life they seemed to lead. It would be fun to stay with them for a while. They thought it would be even *more* fun, when Joan arrived with a truly wonderful meal!

'Home-made veal-and-ham-pie! Stuffed tomatoes! And what a salad – what's in it, Joan? Radishes, cucumber, carrot, beetroot, hard boiled eggs, tomatoes, peas – Joan, you're a marvel! What is the pudding?'

Soon they were all sitting down enjoying themselves, and talking over their adventure. Just as they were finishing, the telephone bell rang. Julian went to answer it. He came back looking thrilled.

'That was the Inspector. They've got all three men! When they got to the pit, one of the men called up for help – said some idiot of a boy or some hoaxer must have taken their rope away. So the police – all in plain-clothes, so that of course the three men suspected nothing – the police let down a rope, and up came the men one by one . . .'

'And were arrested as soon as they popped out of the hole, I suppose!' said George, delighted. 'Oh, I wish I'd been there! What a joke!'

'The Inspector's awfully pleased with us,' said Julian. 'And so is Sir James Lawton-Harrison too, apparently. We're to get a reward – very hush-hush, though. We mustn't say anything about it. There's to be something for each of us.'

'And for Timmy too?' said George at once.

Julian looked round at Timmy. 'Well, I can see what old Timmy ought to ask for,' he said. 'A new cardboard collar. He's scratching his ear to bits!'

George screamed and rushed to bend over Timmy. She lifted a woebegone face. 'Yes! He's scratched so hard he's made his ear bad again. Oh Timmy! You really are a fat-headed dog! Mother! Mother! Timmy's messed up his ear again!'

Her mother looked into the room. 'Oh George, what a pity! I *told* you not to take off that collar till his ear was absolutely healed!'

'It's maddening!' said George. 'Now everyone will laugh at him again.'

'Oh no they won't,' said Julian, and he smiled at George's scowling face. 'Cheer up – it's a very peculiar thing, George – this adventure *began* with Timmy and a cardboard collar – and bless me if it hasn't *ended* with Timmy and a cardboard collar. Three cheers for old Timmy!'

Yes – three cheers for old Timmy! Get your ear well before the next adventure, Tim – you really *can't* wear a cardboard collar again!

FAMOUS FIVE SERIES

FIVE ON A TREASURE ISLAND
FIVE GO ADVENTURING AGAIN
FIVE RUN AWAY TOGETHER
FIVE GO TO SMUGGLER'S TOP
FIVE GO OFF IN A CARAVAN
FIVE ON KIRRIN ISLAND AGAIN
FIVE GO OFF TO CAMP
FIVE GET INTO TROUBLE
FIVE FALL INTO ADVENTURE
FIVE GO ON A HIKE TOGETHER
FIVE HAVE A WONDERFUL TIME
FIVE GO DOWN TO THE SEA
FIVE GO TO MYSTERY MOOR
FIVE HAVE PLENTY OF FUN
FIVE ON A SECRET TRAIL
FIVE GO TO BILLYCOCK HILL
FIVE GET INTO A FIX
FIVE ON FINNISTON FARM
FIVE GO TO DEMON'S ROCKS
FIVE HAVE A MYSTERY TO SOLVE
FIVE ARE TOGETHER AGAIN

SECRET SEVEN SERIES

THE SECRET SEVEN
SECRET SEVEN ADVENTURE
WELL DONE SECRET SEVEN
SECRET SEVEN ON THE TRAIL
GO AHEAD SECRET SEVEN
GOOD WORK SECRET SEVEN
SECRET SEVEN WIN THROUGH
THREE CHEERS SECRET SEVEN
SECRET SEVEN MYSTERY
PUZZLE FOR THE SECRET SEVEN
SECRET SEVEN FIREWORKS
GOOD OLD SECRET SEVEN
SHOCK FOR THE SECRET SEVEN
LOOK OUT SECRET SEVEN
FUN FOR THE SECRET SEVEN

THE ENID BLYTON TRUST
FOR CHILDREN

We hope you have enjoyed the adventures of the children in this book. Please think for a moment about those children who are too ill to do the exciting things you and your friends do.

Help them by sending a donation, large or small, to the **ENID BLYTON TRUST FOR CHILDREN**. The Trust will use all your gifts to help children who are sick or handicapped and need to be made happy and comfortable.

Please send your postal orders or cheques to:

The Enid Blyton Trust for Children,
3rd Floor,
New South Wales House,
15 Adam Street,
The Strand,
London WC2N 6AH

Thank you very much for your help.